A Match Gone Awry

Georgians in Paris

Arlem Hawks

Copyright © 2024 by Arlem Hawks

All rights reserved.

No part of this book may be reproduced in any form or by any electronic or mechanical means, including information storage and retrieval systems, without written permission from the author, except for the use of brief quotations in a book review.

To Rachel McFarland
Thank you for instilling in me a love of France and appreciation of her history, culture, and language.

CHAPTER 1

March 1774
Paris, France

Surely there were more forward things than arriving on the doorstep of the man you intended to marry unannounced and entirely alone. But as Gabrielle d'Amilly glanced around the morning crowds bustling up and down the length of rue Jacob, she couldn't think of many. If the gentleman didn't know she intended to marry him, did that make it more or less forward?

The windows of the street's townhouses glinted in amusement as she scurried through the arched passage into the British embassy's courtyard. Several more rows of windows blinked curiously down, surrounding her like patrons at a theatre awaiting entertainment. Was *he* at one of the windows? The thought stopped Gabrielle in her tracks. The courtyard lay still and quiet, the sounds of the street muted by its walls.

What was she doing? This morning's excursion to visit a gentleman—an English gentleman—might be forward, but it was only one piece of a ridiculously reckless plot that had seemed so right and foolproof last night. Lying in bed in the dark, tears streaking her cheeks, everything had been so clear. Now standing in the middle of a courtyard in the light of morning, eyes scratchy and dry, the plan didn't seem as wise.

A side door creaked open, and a maid hauled a large basin of water out, giving Gabrielle a curious glance. No doubt the embassy did not receive many female callers at this hour. Gabrielle hurried to the main entrance and up the steps. This was not the time to be timid as usual. She pulled back her mitt and rapped on the door. One couldn't achieve a proper knock if her knuckles were muffled by mitts, but the slight chill lingering in the March air wouldn't allow her to leave home without them. She straightened and pulled her mitt back in place, adopting a countenance of cool indifference. She had to pretend she knew what she was doing. Never mind her heart raced like the pealing of the bells of la Notre Dame.

The door opened, revealing a short man in a stark white wig. He looked her up and down, then grumbled something in English.

Zut alors. English. Gabrielle swallowed. Of course the servants would speak English here. She'd have to learn it, too. And quickly, if all went according to plan.

"Monsieur Finch?" She didn't know if she was pronouncing his name correctly. She'd only heard fellow Frenchmen say it.

The short man's scowl only darkened.

"Finch?" she asked again. She grasped the sides of her red petticoat, desperately fighting to keep her tone unconcerned. If only she had an ounce of her stepmother, Élisabeth's, charm. The woman could flirt her way through any door, whether she knew the butler's language or not.

A voice carried from behind the unimpressed servant. She couldn't make out the words, but the friendly tone incited hope. The voice was too weathered to be Monsieur Finch's, but it had to be that of his employer, Lord Stormont, the British ambassador to Paris.

The butler backed away from the door, speaking in an argumentative tone. Then a hand wrapped around the edge of the door and opened it wide.

"Now who has graced us with her presence this morning?" The ambassador's eyes fell on her, and a wide grin split the man's face. She'd never seen him in such a state, his graying hair tightly cropped, no wig, and a banyan haphazardly secured about him. He always dressed carefully and with simple elegance, which endeared him to all of Parisian society despite its penchant for flamboyance.

"Mademoiselle d'Amilly. To what do we owe such pleasure?" he asked in French.

Merci Dieu. What would she have done if the butler had turned her away? Gabrielle curtsied. "*Bonjour*, Lord Stormont." No sense in delay. "I have come to inquire after Monsieur Finch. He seemed to have injured his foot at the ball last evening."

The ambassador's eyebrows pulled together. "Finch is not in."

Her stomach sank. Not in? This early in the day? She'd come early on purpose to catch him before the ambassador sent him all over the city attending to clerical duties. All her forwardness had been for naught. She could practically hear Élisabeth's laughter. *Poor, sweet Gabrielle. You should have consulted me first.*

Gabrielle bit her lip. No. She would never consult that woman on matters of love.

"You needn't fear for Finch, however," Lord Stormont continued, a kindly smile on his face as though he could read her intentions. "He took a guest of ours to visit the gardens of the Tuileries. He seemed well as ever."

The Tuileries! Perhaps there was still a chance to catch him. She glanced down at the watch dangling from a fob at her waist. Élisabeth wished her to attend a gown fitting later that morning. She had time to find Monsieur Finch at the Tuileries and make it home. It wouldn't be time spent alone, but a visit with him was better than no visit. The more occasions she had to spend with him, the better her odds at catching his interest. And with any luck, his heart.

"Thank you, *monseigneur*, I will—"

A boy dashed up the steps, and Gabrielle turned, allowing him room in front of the door.

"Yes, what is it?" Lord Stormont asked. Though he spoke with a decided English accent, his mastery of French was impressive. At least to someone like Gabrielle who had no mastery of any language other than her own.

"Message for Monsieur Finch," the boy said, winded. He held up a folded square of paper. "I'm to give it to him directly."

The ambassador's lips twitched. "Finch is a sought-after man today." He reached for the letter. "I will see that he gets it."

An idea flashed into Gabrielle's mind, and before she could consider it thoughtfully, she blurted, "I can take it."

"That is very kind, mademoiselle, but I would not trouble you," Lord Stormont said.

"It is practically on my way." Not entirely true, but she hoped he wouldn't notice that. Did she sound as desperate as she felt staring at the folded page? "It will be no trouble, I assure you."

The ambassador took the note and slipped the boy a coin from his pocket. He turned it over. "Who sent this?"

"Monsieur la Barre," the boy said.

Lord Stormont snorted. "That can't contain anything of importance, but I will humor you."

Was he talking to Monsieur la Barre or to her? Gabrielle clasped her hands to keep from fidgeting while he waved the messenger away.

Turning back to her, the hint of a laugh escaped him as he nodded once. "Very well. I would be most grateful for your service, mademoiselle."

Gabrielle's face heated despite the cool morning. She ducked her head, willing the brim of her black silk bonnet to hide her blush. No matter how hard she tried, she couldn't carry herself with the confidence of her stepmother. *You are an open book, chérie, and all the world can read it.*

He handed the note to her with a wink. "You'd best be on your way. Not a moment to lose."

It was all Gabrielle could do to keep from running down the steps and back through the archway to her waiting coach. A morning with Monsieur Finch. She urged the coachman to take them to the gardens of the Tuileries with all the speed he could manage through the cobbled streets of Paris. She plopped into her seat and barely contained a giggle of delight as the servant closed the door. This was the start of a new life, free from the follies of her father and his wife. As the coach bumped forward, the towering townhouses of rue Jacob dissolved into daydreams of London, new and fresh and far, far from here.

Harvey Barlow strolled a half step behind his new acquaintance Edward Finch as the man pointed out the architectural beauties of the Tuileries Palace to their left. Of course Harvey enjoyed a classical monstrosity as much as the next man, but this early in the morning he usually preferred a cup of tea, a sweet biscuit, and the melody of ocean waves on a ship's hull. Absent a seaworthy vessel, he would settle for just the tea and biscuit. Perhaps Finch's tour of the Tuileries Gardens would end at a café or tea shop.

"Can you imagine having such grandeur at your disposal and doing nothing with it?" Finch asked, gaze still on the looming palace. He was a friendly chap, obedient and eager to please, like the clerk of an ambassador should be. Or a prized spaniel. Harvey bit back a grin. He couldn't imagine him to be older than twenty-three, which made Harvey at least five years his senior. Experience would eventually take its toll and turn the clerk into a savvy politician.

"It's hard to comprehend having that much wealth," Harvey said, taking in the building's rigid stone columns. If his family had possessed even a fraction of this wealth, he might not have gone to sea. Seventeen children spread the family's finances thinner than his father appreciated.

"Think of what you could do with it, Lieutenant," Finch said, pausing their walk and spreading his arms wide. "The advances in science and philosophy and the arts you could fund."

Harvey simply nodded, not bothering to point out how much monarchies did contribute to those things already, such as employing architects to design and build great palaces that housed art and theatre and scientific discoveries. Finch would learn. "Shall we make for the gardens?" Though there was only meager foliage this time of year, greenery was one of the few things he missed while at sea. That and a good pastry shop.

"Yes, of course." Finch pivoted, the palace seemingly forgotten. "I think you will enjoy this."

They turned down a path lined with stately rows of trees in an English style. For all their countries' rivalry, Britain and France certainly loved to borrow from each other. The trees were just getting a fresh batch of leaves after the long winter, enough to partially obscure the walkways. A grand pond with a fountain at its center lay at the end of the path, but they hadn't turned the water on this early in the spring.

"Will you be without a ship for long?" Finch asked.

By Jove, he hoped not, but there was an excess of officers when England was not at war with France. "We shall see," Harvey said, adjusting the collar of his navy coat. He wore his undress coat out of habit, but perhaps he should take on a less noticeable appearance. Despite currently having a truce, the French may not like to see a member of the British Royal Navy parading through their streets.

And who knew how long that truce would last? The threat of war loomed over the Atlantic, which was why Admiral Pratt had sent Harvey on this assignment to Paris. Contention had risen in the colonies after the utter chaos of dumping tea in the harbor in December, and Britain's threat of strict new laws had only made it worse. The colonies would be seeking allies, and who better to recruit than Great Britain's closest enemy? Harvey was to check the pulse of France's opinion toward the wayward colonists, meeting with the admiral's list of contacts throughout the city. If they had to prepare for war on two fronts, Admiral Pratt wanted to be ready to push for the rank advancements and commands for his loyal officers.

Pale spring light painted the pond's white stone a buttery yellow. Birds hopped about it as though looking for water, flying off in a huff when their hopes weren't realized.

Finch clasped his hands behind his back. "I suppose in all your waiting for an assignment, you might find yourself a wife."

A wife. Heat drained from Harvey's face. That was in the works, all part of Admiral Pratt's plans to get his difficult daughter married and favorite lieutenant a promotion. An admiral's son-in-law awaiting advancement to post-captain would be of higher priority than an unattached lieutenant in the politics of the Royal Navy. Harvey would be just the first of a collection of loyal and competent captains Admiral Pratt hoped would bring in prize money from captured ships. With good captains under him and an admiral's hefty share of each prize, Admiral Pratt would be in position to earn a fine fortune should war break out with the colonies. Harvey would also profit, of course, so he could hardly complain. With that as the goal, what was all this dread?

He cleared his throat. "I am in contact with a gentleman over his daughter's hand. An admiral, as it were."

Finch's face lit up. "Truly?" A romantic. He should have guessed. "My sincerest congratulations, then."

Harvey forced a smile. "Nothing is settled yet. Nor is it public, so I would appreciate discretion."

"Oh, yes. Of course." Finch quickened his pace. "Do you know her well, then? Her father being in the navy and all."

Please, not the questions. Harvey removed his cocked

hat, smoothing out his light brown hair before settling the hat back on his head. "Her father I know well, but I have seen her only a few times before."

"How intriguing. What is she like? Will you get on well?"

Harvey swallowed. How he hoped. "She seems to be a likable enough young lady. Fashionable. Quick witted." Vain as a peacock and none too impressed with her father's plans, despite the admiral believing she was excited.

Finch sighed, staring wistfully through the rows of trees. "Oh, to be in that era of my life. I cannot wait for the day I have the income to find someone to be the lady of my humble abode. I haven't the fortune to appeal to most families yet."

"Lord Stormont said you owned a townhouse in London. You're hardly penniless," Harvey said encouragingly.

"Yes. Quite small, but it suits my mother and me. I do not know if it would suit a young lady of class."

There was something to be said for small abodes. Harvey owned a little cottage in Sussex which he loved dearly, but he did not think Miss Pratt would appreciate the quaintness or remoteness. The admiral had already hinted at the need to sell it and buy something larger once prize money came in.

"The gardens are rather scarce of people," he remarked, eager to be done with the subject of marriage. "I take it this isn't a popular place at eight o'clock in the morning on a Tuesday."

"Usually it is. Perhaps...Tuesday!" Finch jerked his watch from his pocket. "Gracious! I was to meet with Monsieur Borde this morning. It completely slipped my mind."

Relief flooded Harvey. "You should go then. I will wander back to the embassy." And if he happened upon a café, or better yet a *pâtisserie*, on his way, all the better. He wanted to forget this talk of marriage and the future in the flaky depths of something sweet.

"Will you remember the way?" The clerk started in the direction of the street.

"I've learned a thing or two about navigation in my years at sea." The River Seine bordered the Tuileries Gardens to the south, and not far beyond was rue Jacob and Lord Stormont's residence. He'd consider himself a poor excuse for a sailor if he couldn't locate the nearest body of water through these gardens.

Finch laughed, walking backward to continue conversing. "Of course. I should not count a navy lieutenant helpless. I will see you this evening." He hurried off, arms pumping.

Oh, to have that man's energy and enthusiasm. Harvey lowered his head and took a path leading through a large stretch of trees. Once he'd been as eager for marriage as Finch. His father had made sure to cure him of that. Add in being at the navy's beck and call, and he couldn't see much joy in the prospect. Marriage was a duty, and he would faithfully fulfill his obligation.

But as he ambled through the soft Parisian morning, with wind tickling the branches and a peaceful glow illuminating the quiet footpaths, a small part of him still hoped that marriage would be so much more.

CHAPTER 2

Gabrielle had tried to keep composed with the air of a determined—but not desperate—woman having an important goal, but as she hurried through the gardens with no sight of Monsieur Finch, her pace quickened. She'd made it all the way from the southeast entrance to the northwest entrance and hadn't glimpsed anyone who looked even remotely like him. The sun crept ever higher and the note weighed heavier in her hand. She had to find him to deliver this, even if she didn't get much time with him.

The slap of her shoes on the gravelly path filled her ears, underscored by her labored breathing. Where was that man? If she was late to the dress fitting, Élisabeth wouldn't let her hear the end of it.

A flash of sapphire coat slipped through the branches. The same color Monsieur Finch's coat had been on the day they first met, drinking tea in Lord Stormont's salon. Seeing it again brought a smile to her lips. It looked so well on him now, the way it hugged his shoulders and trim frame. He was walking the path that ran parallel to her own, divided by a row of trees. Gabrielle sent a prayer of thanks heavenward and practically sprinted toward him. Perhaps she'd have more than just a moment with him before she had to leave.

"Monsieur?"

Monsieur Finch did not turn.

"Monsieur!" She waved the note in the air. "Monsieur, I have a message for you of utmost importance."

To her relief, the man stopped, allowing her to cut the distance. "How do you do, Monsieur Finch? Is your foot recovered?"

He cocked his head, clearly not recognizing her through the mostly-bare branches.

"It is Gabrielle d'Amilly." Had he forgotten they'd danced only last night? No, certainly not. Monsieur Finch might not have the most excellent of memories, but he couldn't have forgotten her after several meetings. Last night he'd seemed to enjoy dancing with her. She slipped through the trees. "I am very happy to…"

A pair of brown eyes peered out from under arched brows on a square-jawed face that was decidedly not Monsieur Finch's. Rather than blue silk, deep blue wool covered his shoulders. White lapels ran down his chest, speckled with anchor-embossed gold buttons.

"…see you." Gabrielle gulped, freezing with her arm extended toward him. The note flicked in the faint morning breeze.

"If you are looking for Monsieur Finch, he was obliged to visit Monsieur Borde." The man spoke with a pronounced English accent—deep and sophisticated. He studied her, and for a moment it seemed as though those brown eyes could see straight through her.

She slowly retracted the note. "Excuse me, monsieur. I

mistook you." This must be the guest Lord Stormont was talking about. She retreated a step, wishing the uncovered branches could swallow her. Had he seen her earnestness? How could he not have? It would only be too obvious she had intentions toward Monsieur Finch.

"Do you have a note for him? May I deliver it to him on your behalf?" He was a military man, no doubt. He stood properly straight like the mast of a ship, his light brown hair tied in a simple but tidy queue.

"It isn't mine," she said quickly. "It arrived at the embassy not long ago and I offered to bring it to him." Insisted, rather.

Curiosity flashed across his face. "I am very sorry to not be Monsieur Finch." He was more perceptive than the ambassador's clerk. Gabrielle resisted covering her face with her hands. She should not have admitted she'd tried to call at the embassy so early in the morning. Tearing her gaze away, she focused on the pond a ways behind them.

"I can return it to the embassy for you."

"*Merci,* monsieur." She shoved the note toward him, suddenly wishing to be rid of it so she could flee home. The sooner she left, the better chance this fine English gentleman forgot her sorry existence. She could drown her mortification in trying to fawn over her stepmother's new clothes.

His fingers brushed hers as he took the folded paper, gave her a smiling nod, and put it in his breast pocket. "I shall see it safely to him, mademoiselle." His tone hinted he knew what she was about, and her stomach sank to her shoes.

Just as she was gathering her strength to thank him and run, a voice sounded from the path behind her. "Lieutenant

Barlow?" It was feminine and energetic and vaguely familiar. "When did you return to Paris?"

They both turned toward the greeting, and Gabrielle's breath caught. Madame Necker! The woman, who was in her late thirties, drifted over to them with a poise Gabrielle could only dream of possessing. Madame Necker was hostess of one of the legendary Parisian salons. Each week she welcomed into her home artists and authors and some of the most elite *philosophes* France had ever seen. Gabrielle had been trying to determine a way to secure an invitation to the mostly male gatherings, since Monsieur Finch spoke so enthusiastically about attending them. She'd read so much of the *philosophes'* works, full of deep thoughts on life. Reading was one of the things that kept her sane after her father practically exiled himself to their country estate and left her in town with Élisabeth. How did this English lieutenant know a famous *saloniste*?

The woman extended her hand in his direction, and he bowed gallantly over it. "I arrived just last evening," he said. So that was why he hadn't attended the ball with the rest of the ambassador's party. Her family frequented parties with the English ambassador often enough that she would have noticed him if he'd been there long.

"Then you haven't missed one of my little gatherings yet. You must come Friday. I insist."

Little gatherings. That were known throughout the city. Gabrielle smoothed the front of her petticoat. Should she try to disappear while he was distracted? Or... An idea tickled her mind. Had fate presented her an invaluable opportunity?

Lieutenant Barlow chuckled, a rich baritone sound that seemed to roll through the gardens. "Finch has already insisted I come. I assure you, I would not miss it."

Madame Necker smiled. "If I remember correctly, we were a sorry gathering the last time you came. I promise to have the best conversation this week. And every week that you are here. Are you here for long?"

"I will be here for a month," he said. "Until April the eighteenth."

"*Tant mieux*. You ran off too quickly on your last visit." Madame Necker swatted playfully at his hand. "We shall enjoy each moment." The woman turned her gaze in Gabrielle's direction, and Gabrielle straightened instantly. "Now, who is this lovely creature?"

Lieutenant Barlow gestured in her direction, panic flitting across his face. "Allow me to introduce Mademoiselle—"

"D'Amilly," Gabrielle finished quickly, curtsying. Madame Necker was not *noblesse* by any means. In fact one might argue that Gabrielle's parents were closer to nobility than the Neckers, but being the influential wife of an equally influential banker demanded respect. "Our family currently resides in your former home, madame. The Hôtel d'Hallwyll."

Madame Necker's face softened. Élisabeth always commented on her plain features—light hair carefully powdered, gray eyes, and a pleasant yet unaffected visage —but Gabrielle could not call her plain. Not with that knowing twinkle in her eye. "*Bien sûr*, I thought you looked familiar. How are your parents?"

Still trying to purchase a *lettre de noblesse* to give them a noble title. They had already purchased a noble's land and started styling themselves as nobility. "Quite well, *merci*," Gabrielle said, attempting to sound as uninteresting as possible. She wanted to avoid speaking of her father and his wife. Once, she and her father had been the closest of friends, but that all faded when Élisabeth entered their world.

"I saw your stepmother's cousins and brother recently," Madame Necker said, lips twisting into a semblance of a smile.

That could not have been pleasant. "Which ones?"

"Monsieur Rouvroy and the de Vintimilles."

Ah, yes. Rouvroy was married to the niece of the king's minister and prided himself in knowing everything that went on at court. The de Vintimilles were relations of the king's illegitimate son and loved to flaunt their connection. None of them particularly liked Gabrielle's family, but Élisabeth loved to invite them to everything. She felt it elevated her status. The lieutenant studied her carefully, interest clear in his eyes. Did he know them?

Gabrielle did not want his or Madame Necker's opinions of those relatives to reflect on her. It would be best to change the subject immediately. "Will the ambassador be in attendance this week? And his staff? Monsieur Finch and the others?" Imagine, sitting in a salon with the *philosophes*, listening to and conversing with Monsieur Finch on a settee in a quiet corner. Surely for a scholar such as he, there could be no more certain place to fall in love than a Parisian salon.

Lieutenant Barlow raised an eyebrow. *Ciel.* They'd already spoken about that. This was why Élisabeth teased her whenever they were in public. She couldn't keep her head from getting muddled. The lieutenant's attention was not helping. She kept her focus on Madame Necker, or she knew her face would flush. If he hadn't noticed her intrigue with Monsieur Finch before, he surely would have noticed it by now.

"Lord Stormont and Monsieur Finch will be there," the woman said. "Monsieur Finch is a dear. I do enjoy his enthusiasm and conversation. What a fine young Englishman he is."

Gabrielle could not help the corners of her mouth ticking upward. Monsieur Finch was a fine young man made finer by his possession of a little townhouse in London far from the mess of Parisian society. While the thought of leaving the land she knew, of never seeing the lush countryside of her childhood again, terrified her, there wasn't any place in France she could go where her stepmother wouldn't try to find and benefit off of her. "Do you have large gatherings most Fridays?" Was her interest too obvious?

"Not lately." Madame Necker sighed, folding her mitt-covered hands over her violet cloak. "With Grimm and Diderot in Russia, we have a much smaller company, I'm afraid. And Diderot refuses to write to inform us of all the happenings of Catherine II's court, so we do not have letters to discuss. Our lieutenant will be a much-needed refreshment to our usual company."

What more could she say beyond outright asking to come? Gabrielle fiddled with the fichu about her neck. That sort of forwardness would only repel the *saloniste*. "How fortunate our lieutenant has come to Paris, then." As soon as she realized what she'd said, she bit her lip. *Our* lieutenant! She'd met him ten minutes ago. Madame Necker would think they were long acquaintances. And the handsome lieutenant would think her a shameless flirt like her stepmother.

He cleared his throat. Yes, he did think her a flirt. Why did she do this? No matter how much effort she spent, she could not keep herself from these situations. Best if she just curtsied and left them to their friendly chat.

"Might I be terribly bold, madame?" he asked.

Madame Necker laughed. "I'd expect nothing less from you. That is why we like you."

After this little aside, Gabrielle would make her apologies and bolt. She just needed a slight break in the conversation.

"Might we include Mademoiselle d'Amilly in our gathering this Friday evening?"

Gabrielle froze. Had she heard him correctly?

"She is such an admirer of the *philosophes*' work."

She shot him a look. What was he doing? He didn't know that. Of course she'd read many of the encyclopedias Diderot had published, but she hadn't mentioned that in their short interaction.

Madame Necker opened her mouth as though to speak, then paused. She took in Gabrielle's appearance for several moments. Gabrielle didn't know whether to return her gaze or look elsewhere, which meant she resorted to an awkward combination.

"Yes, do bring her along," Madame Necker said. "We are celebrating the publication of Madame d'Épinay's book, *Conversations d'Émilie*. It would do well to have another woman in our midst."

Gabrielle's heart leaped. She hardly believed the words. *She* had an invitation to Madame Necker's salon? She hadn't thought it possible. A whole evening of intelligent conversation and hanging onto Monsieur Finch's every word. His nearly undivided attention, being one of only a few females in attendance. She'd nearly given up on the possibility of such an opportunity, and now this stranger had secured it in a moment.

"Ah, there is Madame Geoffrin," Madame Necker said, peering through the line of trees. "I did not expect to see her here this morning. You will both excuse me. I must bid her good day. Until Friday." The *saloniste* curtsied to them with another odd glance, then strode confidently away.

Lieutenant Barlow didn't return his cocked hat to his head after coming out of his bow to Madame Necker, but turned to Gabrielle and gave her one as well. "I believe I must continue on my way, mademoiselle. Would you be so kind as to point me in the direction of a *pâtisserie*?"

Her head was too muddled to think of one. From mortification to elation in so short a time had left her dizzy. "You want a *pâtisserie*?"

"Do you know of them? Shops crowded with morsels of flaky dough, custard, jelly, honey, sultanas, currants, all best with a healthy coating of sugar?"

Gabrielle scowled, arms akimbo. "I know what a *pâtisserie* is."

The lieutenant tilted his head. "The look on your face suggested perhaps you didn't."

The look on her face. She swiped a hand across it. The ghost of a grin touched his lips. They pinched together as though he were trying not to laugh. It was contagious. Gabrielle drew in a deep breath to keep from following suit. She'd already looked too much the fool this morning.

"I am partial to Stohrer's on rue Montorgueil." She pointed east. "If you turn left onto rue du Louvre, it will take you there, though it is a bit of a walk."

He gracefully rested his hat on his head and straightened. How had she mistaken him for Monsieur Finch? He was significantly taller. "I have time to spare in order to secure the finest pastries in Paris. *Merci, mademoiselle*. I shall have Finch in his best form for you Friday evening. And I shall be sure to deliver the note, of course."

Gabrielle's stomach lurched as the lieutenant marched away in pursuit of his pastries. Did he truly know? Or was she simply inventing that he had caught on to her interest in his friend?

She watched him leave the gardens, the memory of his grin still pressing on her mind. He had a nice smile, one that would have made her feel warm and comfortable if not for the humiliation of the idea that he had guessed her plan. She turned and trudged back in the direction of her coach. How had he guessed it? The question would eat at her like moths at an old garment.

When she arrived at the coach, the coachman hopped down to open the door. She put a foot on the step, then turned to stare in the direction Lieutenant Barlow had gone. She couldn't see him through the trees and increasing stream of wealthy Parisians. "Take me to Stohrer's," she said, then slipped into the coach before she could take it back. She wouldn't let the question fester. There were too many other festering things in her life.

CHAPTER 3

P aris certainly wasn't short on palaces. Harvey glanced about the street before darting through a break in the line of carriages, heading away from the Louvre. Of course, it wasn't just Paris. London had its own mess of extravagance, but that was why Harvey didn't care for the large cities. Too much bustle and carrying on in order to please the moneyed leaders.

"*Attendez!*"

A carriage turned onto the street he'd just entered, and he moved to the side to avoid it. They wouldn't be calling for him. He knew so few French people beyond the circles in which the ambassador and his employees moved on the regular, despite having visited the ambassador on a few occasions. But he didn't fancy getting run over by a pair of horses, French or English.

That wasn't entirely true. If he had to be run over, it had better be by English steeds. A lifetime at war made it difficult to accept any French victory, even an equine one.

The horses slowed and stopped just beside him, a pair of fine green eyes watching him intently through the lowered window of the coach. "*Attendez*, lieutenant. Wait a moment."

"Mademoiselle d'Amilly," he said, bowing as though they hadn't just parted company. "I did not expect to see you again so soon." It was only too easy to see that her mind was working at breakneck speed, a flush on her cheeks.

The greeting was ignored. "May we take you to Stohrer's *pâtisserie*?" she asked.

Not a woman to muddle in pleasantries. How would Finch take it, being all pleasantries? "I do not mind the walk," he said, but she stared at him so intently that he didn't dare refuse. "However, I would be most grateful for the company." He climbed in, not waiting for the coachman to get the door for him. Inside, Mademoiselle d'Amilly fidgeted with her petticoat, which was a shade of red far too loud for her delicate coloring. The matching jacket was a mess of lace at the sleeves and neck that hardly suited. From what he had heard of the Rouvroys and de Vintimilles from the ambassador, perhaps it fit. They were notorious social climbers who liked to pretend themselves above their station, but this young lady did not seem to fit that description from the morning's interactions.

Harvey settled his hat and walking stick beside him. "To what do I owe—"

"Why did you request my inclusion at the salon?"

The coach rolled forward, and Harvey had to brace himself in order to not get flung across the coach into the mademoiselle. "Do you not wish to attend?"

She leaned forward. "No, no, no. I mean yes. Yes, I do wish to attend. I only wonder how you knew that and why you asked."

Beneath her bonnet, her hair was lightly powdered

enough for a dark brown to seep through like chocolate puffs dusted with sugar. She didn't wear it styled as lofty as most high class women of his acquaintance, though it *was* only a Tuesday morning. Plenty of better opportunities for hair of greater heights. Better opportunities that included her introducing him to her relatives? Those climbing the social ladder were the best at divulging information. They took too much pride in knowing things others didn't. Could he find an excuse for her to introduce him to these flamboyant relations?

"It seemed…" Should he speak the truth? She'd be embarrassed. But something in her intense stare made him think she'd prefer it to empty niceties. "You seemed very intent on meeting Finch this morning and quite disappointed when I was not said gentleman. I thought to make it up to you by giving you another opportunity."

"Oh." She sat back, turning toward the window. "Was it terribly obvious?"

Harvey chuckled. "Your face said many things your lips did not."

She closed her eyes and rubbed her brow, muttering something that he did not catch. The young woman's mouth puckered in frustration.

Harvey rested his hand on the golden handle of his walking stick. "Do you…" Blast, what was the word in French? He'd never used the language to speak about this sort of thing before. He didn't want to be overly blunt. "Do you fancy Finch?"

The young woman blinked, her brow creased.

That phrase clearly didn't translate. "Do you…love Monsieur Finch?" Love was too strong a word, but he couldn't think of a better way to say it.

"Do I love him?" Mademoiselle d'Amilly's already pink

cheeks deepened a shade. She twisted her hands together, examining the embroidery on her mitts. "I...I want to."

"You want to be in love with Finch?" But she wasn't already? How curiously odd.

She straightened primly, waving. "I've said too much. We are here. Go enjoy your pastries, Lieutenant." The carriage slowed and stopped beside a sign that read "Pâtisserie Stohrer" in gold lettering. Through the shop window a small array of tables and chairs peeked through. So it was a tea house of sorts as well. He couldn't complain about that.

Harvey didn't budge. A young French woman of good money, if not fashion, wanting to be in love with an English ambassador's clerk. That wasn't supposed to happen for quite a few reasons. He certainly wouldn't get the story at Madame Necker's Friday evening with Finch nearby. This could be his only opportunity to hear the story and perhaps ask her the favor.

"Will you join me, mademoiselle?"

She eyed him. "At the *pâtisserie*?"

"Of course."

"I've already eaten breakfast."

Harvey shrugged. "It is always a good time for a pastry, I've found." The coachman opened the door, and Harvey grabbed his hat and walking stick. He descended, clamped his hat down on his head, then turned to extend a hand to the young lady. "Come. A little sweetness will give you the vitality you need to face the rest of the day."

Her hand hesitantly slid into his, her fingers peeking out of her mitts cool and soft. She allowed him to help her down. "I cannot stay long," she said. "My stepmother expects me at a dress fitting."

"Ah, having new clothes is nice." And good heavens, she could use something that fit her. This ensemble was made of the finest silk, but it looked like it was made to suit another woman entirely.

She tugged at the bodice and attempted to flatten a wrinkle. With her bonnet and hair, she was nearly as tall as he was. The bodice looked short for her willowy frame. "Unfortunately the fitting is not my own. It is for a new gown for my stepmother."

"I see." A pity. She did not look comfortable in what she currently wore.

Harvey pushed open the door to the tinkle of a bell above the doorframe. A sweet, warm aroma, touched with a pinch of spice, plowed into him. He paused on the threshold to drink it in, and Mademoiselle d'Amilly hit his back with enough force to knock her backward. He turned and snatched her arm, as quick and sure as he caught a ship's ratline when going aloft. She stayed on her feet, apologizing rapidly.

He held up a hand. "No need to apologize. It was I who stopped suddenly." He greeted the shopkeeper, then led her to a table beside the window. He pulled out her chair for her, which she sat on quickly before he could help push it in. It was much too far from the table to be comfortable. Biting back a grin, he assisted her as she scooted once, twice, three times to position herself at the right distance. The chair's legs moaned loudly with each motion, drawing glances from the few other patrons. She hadn't had many gentlemen help her sit, had she?

Harvey took the seat across from her. The shop had a striped wallpaper in pale blue and green, trimmed with buttery yellow molding. Gilded mirrors adorned the walls, making the space appear much more open than it was. Twinkling reflections of candles winked in the mirrors' polished surfaces. It wasn't Michelson's no-nonsense and incredibly British pastry shop in Sussex, but the *pâtisserie* had a warmth about it that made him comfortable despite how far he was from home. Harvey motioned to the man at the counter, who nodded in his direction and turned back to the customer he was assisting.

"What is it you want?" she asked when he'd settled.

He rubbed his hands together. "One of everything, of course, but I will settle for whatever is their specialty."

"That isn't what I—"

"Will you have coffee? Tea?" he asked. "Perhaps join me in something sweet?" It would give him a minute to collect his thoughts.

"I am not very hungry." The young woman eyed him suspiciously.

Harvey cocked his head. "Come, there must be something. Can a person not be hungry for pastries?"

She looked at him long and hard before sighing. "*D'accord*, I will take a madeleine and a little coffee."

Harvey smiled. There. He'd thought he could convince her. "Excellent. What is their best treat?"

"I do quite like the *baba*," she said. "Monsieur Stohrer is known for developing it while he served the king of Poland."

"Then that is what I shall have." The shopkeeper, a man balding on top but with enough hair around the sides for a queue, approached and greeted them. "We would like madeleines and a serving of the *baba*, if you please. Coffee for the mademoiselle, and I will take tea."

"How very English of you," she said as the man left to retrieve their order.

Harvey laughed. "We British must be predictable once in a while, or we cannot take you by surprise."

"You have already taken me by surprise enough this

morning," she mumbled, watching the shopkeeper select their pastries. "What is it you want from me?"

Harvey folded his hands atop the table between them. "I find it very interesting that a young lady such as yourself would desire to fall in love with a man such as Finch."

She winced and fussed with her hair. "Is he not worthy of such attention?"

"Finch? Oh, no, of course he is perfectly amiable and loyal and of great character. But..." How did he say this? Truthfully, of course. "Finch is by no means wealthy." Not someone who could support an aristocratic wife.

"I care nothing about that," she said, shaking her head.

She said that now, but would life in a London townhouse, away from her native land, her family, and all the wealth that they enjoyed change her mind? "That is very romantic of you. And yet, it sounds as though you are trying to fall in love with him, rather than allowing it to happen naturally." He tapped his finger against the table. "That is the part that I am struggling to make sense of."

She worried her lower lip, face going pale. Was she weighing how much of the truth she dared to disclose to him? She looked like a house maid caught sneaking out of the cellar with a bottle of wine.

"Of course, you do not have to tell me your secrets, mademoiselle. I only thought that if I knew the nature of your feelings toward my friend..." Acquaintance? He hardly knew the man. "...perhaps I could know how best to help encourage Finch in a desirable direction."

"I..."

The man arrived with a tray, from which he retrieved their drinks and pastries. He placed a plate with a little pile of shell-shaped cakes in front of Mademoiselle d'Amilly and a glistening, syrup-drenched cake topped with cream in front of Harvey. His mouth watered. The shopkeeper bowed and retreated.

Harvey rapidly plucked up a fork and scooped off a hearty bite.

"Why would you want to assist me?" she asked.

He paused, bite nearly to his mouth. Was it fascination over her situation? The hope that she could arrange a meeting that would help him gather the information the admiral sought? Something in her eyes saddened him. They were the eyes of someone who didn't think highly of herself to the point she only wanted escape, not happiness. Perhaps with the arrangement of his own questionably blissful engagement on the horizon, he wanted to see someone happy in her situation.

Throat suddenly dry, he lowered his fork and took up his tea instead. "Finch is a good man, and I would love to see him settled." It wasn't a terrible lie. He did think Finch would make a decent husband.

"He is a good man," she agreed quietly. Clinks of forks on plates nearly drowned her out. "I need a good man, one who is kind and amicable, to get me out of here." She flinched after saying it, as though she regretted it.

Just as he thought. She was trying to escape. "Surely there are better ways to leave Paris than to marry yourself off."

Mademoiselle d'Amilly ducked her head, eyes on her skirt. She hadn't touched her coffee or madeleines. "Not for me. My parents wouldn't dream of my leaving. My father and his wife, mostly his wife, are attempting to secure a *lettre de noblesse* and elevate our station, and she wants a wealthy connection added to the family for financial favors."

She was part of one of those families. Harvey's spirits

sank. He should have guessed it from the description of her relatives he'd received. His father would have said the parents were right to utilize whatever resources they had. And though he was going into a resource marriage himself, a part of him couldn't stand the thought.

"My father has already purchased Amilly," she continued, "which used to belong to a baron who could not pay his debts. When he married my stepmother, she wanted nothing more than to be styled in a noble manner. For her, his land was the greatest of his attractions."

What a sorry situation. Thank heavens Harvey's land wasn't his greatest attraction. Not that he had many attractions beyond being Admiral Pratt's favorite lieutenant and having the potential to win a fair amount of prizes in war. To any other family, he would be as lowly as Finch. Harvey lifted the fork again and took his bite. The rich tones of wine from the sticky syrup made him pause. The cake was delicate and moist, not unlike a tea cake. Ah, yes. This would do nicely to satiate his hunger.

Mademoiselle d'Amilly tensed. "I've said too much," she said, voice pinched.

Harvey waved a hand and smiled warmly. How could he not with such sweetness before him? "Everything you've spoken is safe with me. I'm but an English lieutenant who will soon leave the country."

She regarded him, a thoughtful look on her face. Then she plucked up one of the madeleines. "You've just arrived and you are already talking about leaving? Are you so put out by Paris?"

He scooped up another bite of the *baba*. "Certainly not. I am quite content with Paris at the moment, but I have things to attend to at home." Marriage among them. Pity they couldn't combine the effort of making a match, since they were both working toward the same goal. She would likely be happier with him than Miss Pratt would be, since Mademoiselle d'Amilly didn't care about wealth. She couldn't help get him a promotion, though. He slipped the bite into his mouth. And the international nature of such a marriage could bring its own complications. Had she considered that with Finch?

"Will you not need their permission to marry?" he asked. "I seem to recall needing it in France regardless of your age." Although if they waited until they got to England, she wouldn't have an issue as long as she was older than twenty-one. The Church of England didn't take kindly to Catholic marriages anyway.

She chewed her madeleine with a frown. "I will have to think of something. After I've procured him."

Harvey nodded sagely. "Procured him." He'd be offended on Finch's behalf, but a man of Finch's status should be flattered to be considered someone worth procuring.

The mademoiselle choked, seizing a napkin and burying her face in it as she coughed. "That isn't..."

Harvey tried not to laugh through her coughing. He took another bite. Heavens, this *baba* was sweet.

"I didn't mean..." She cleared her throat, fixing him with a stern look through watery eyes.

He waved his fork. "You don't need to explain yourself." After all, his father had taught him marriage was a business transaction. One procured goods in business transactions. A weight settled in his stomach, driving away any more thought of eating. He set down his fork and pushed the plate away. "What are your plans for this procuring?"

Her cheeks pinked. "I thought to put myself in his company as often as possible."

Harvey nodded. "A good start. What else?"

She blinked, then looked away.

That was it? Harvey attempted to hide his dismay through a long sip of tea—so long someone might have mistaken it for a swig. "We shall see how far I can help you get by the time I leave."

"Before you leave?" Was that hope in her voice? He hadn't heard much hope since the start of their conversation. He liked the way it sounded, the way it brightened and strengthened the rich tones of her voice. And he liked how his own heart lifted at the sound. Neither of them were on the path to make a love match, but perhaps with a romantic like Finch she had a chance. "I still do not understand why you wish to help me. We've only just met."

He shrugged, taking another drink while he scrambled for an answer. "You clearly need help from someone outside the situation, and I need something to occupy my time while the ambassador is busy." Not that he wouldn't have plenty to keep him busy, trying to meet with prominent members of Parisian society. Interviewing people like the *philosophes* at Madame Necker's gatherings to gauge public opinion. But here was a task not tied to war and the navy. Something he could do for this young woman that would also lighten the load of cares he'd been shouldering lately.

"That is very kind of you." Suspicion touched her eyes again. Was she not used to someone wanting to help her?

"I have heard quite a lot about your stepmother's relatives," he admitted. "I am anxious to meet them, if it would not be too much trouble."

"Not at all," she said. "I would not wish to meet them myself, but if that is your wish, I have that small thing in my power."

"They seem to be odd people," Harvey said. "I enjoy

making such connections." It's why Madame Necker's philosophes fascinated him, with all their exuberant personalities.

"My stepmother is hosting a card party in a few weeks, and I know she will invite them. That should be before your departure."

"Excellent! That is most kind." He smiled and reached his hand across the table. "In the meantime, we'll win over that Englishman for you."

She didn't shake his hand, but folded her arms. "I seem to be getting a greater part of the bargain."

"On the contrary, it is I who has had all the luck," he said. "I am meeting interesting people and playing the part of matchmaker." And getting vital information for his report to Admiral Pratt, keeping him in the man's good graces and readying them to snatch a promotion. "I am also enjoying a rather delicious pastry and cup of tea. What is lesser about any of that?"

She regarded him, then a little laugh escaped her and she swept up another previously unwanted madeleine.

"How very, very English of you."

CHAPTER 4

Gabrielle slipped through the front door, expecting Élisabeth to be impatiently pacing the vestibule, but not even a footman stood in the empty hall. Had her stepmother fired another servant? She hoped not. Abrupt termination of employment was an infallible way to ruin a day. Gown fittings for someone with far too many gowns came in close behind.

She closed the door and immediately voices assaulted her. Gabrielle paused, wincing as the intensity of the sounds battered against her mind. Why did her stepmother's talking always make her want to hide under the covers of her bed like a frightened child?

The noise carried from the breakfast room, and Gabrielle slid her feet forward, taking care not to knock her thick wooden heels against the floor. Curiosity prevented her from removing her cloak, mitts, and bonnet first.

"I do not understand why you are going to so much expense to host a card party when you've no money to spare." Whose voice was that? It was feminine and cold, but that could describe a good number of her stepmother's family. Gabrielle paused, tucking herself behind the doorframe to not be seen.

"I must host my spring card party," Élisabeth whined. "You know I must. It is the talk of the city."

Her stepmother's guest snorted, and Gabrielle had to agree. No one would realize she'd failed to host an event that had only happened twice. Was that Madame de Vintimille, the cousin who enjoyed Élisabeth's company only because it reinforced her own superiority of position and character?

"You've already spent your stepdaughter's dowry paying off your debts. You have nothing left."

Gabrielle bit her lip, trying to banish the panic that had risen when she first heard about the situation. A line from one of Diderot's works popped into her head. *There are things I cannot force. I must adjust.*

Adjusting was not simple. She closed her eyes, wishing she could adjust her life so she was anywhere but here. The secret of her father and stepmother's disservice echoed with a sharp pang in her heart. It hurt worse that her father had allowed it. The fact that Élisabeth had spent such a sum should not have come as a surprise. How did one adjust to a situation like this?

"If you keep collecting credit, you'll go to the debtors' prison rather than purchasing your *lettre de noblesse*." It was most certainly Madame de Vintimille. She wanted Élisabeth to become noble so she wouldn't have to endure the embarrassment of being seen with a family member of such humble status.

"That is why we have to get Gabrielle married. And soon. To a rich man. If she keeps growing like this, she'll be taller than the men, and they will not look at her. Not to mention she is near to losing her bloom."

Never mind Élisabeth hadn't married until well past Gabrielle's twenty-three years. Gabrielle rubbed her eyes. And she hadn't grown in at least seven years, not since Élisabeth joined the family. She was tall, it was true, but there were men who liked that.

"Have you seen how poorly my clothing fits her?" Élisabeth said. "Alas, we cannot spare the money to get her new clothing."

Only money for Élisabeth's clothing. Speaking of which, if they waited much longer, they would be terribly late to the fitting. Unless her stepmother had canceled it, which would be a blessing.

"Were you not planning a gown fitting for this morning?" Madame de Vintimille asked as though sensing Gabrielle's thoughts.

"We have to finish this guest list before we leave, because I must get it to the calligrapher today. The guests need time to make their plans and cancel those things that interfere."

She should act now to get Lieutenant Barlow on the list. If Élisabeth was flustered, she'd be more likely to give in. Gabrielle squared her shoulders, straightened her gown, and walked serenely into the room. For a moment, neither of the other women looked up. Her stepmother's blonde hair, powdered stark white, was piled high atop her head, and she'd chosen a very pale complexion that morning. Usually such dramatic maquillage was reserved for evening events. Gabrielle walked around the side of the table to take an empty chair, and only then did Élisabeth notice her.

"*Sacré bleu*, but you took an age to return. What were you up to all morning?" The woman took a monstrous bite of the roll in her hand, butter spreading over her brightly rouged lips. She held up a finger. "The Longuevilles. We must invite them. Oh, and Monsieur de Goncourt."

A chill ran over Gabrielle's arms. How dare she invite the man who had helped cause so much grief. Word of Élisabeth's liaison had spread through Paris, humiliating Gabrielle's father and sending him permanently to the country. The woman did not care and still continued to dally with the fop. To say it reflected poorly on Gabrielle was an understatement.

"Is that wise?" Madame de Vintimille asked. She was older than Élisabeth by a few years, but the dissatisfied frown made her look decades older. Light gray hair in an extravagant style and an abundance of lace didn't help make her look wealthier, as Gabrielle was sure she intended. If anything, it made her look like someone of less fortune attempting to look wealthier with ostentation.

Élisabeth ignored her cousin. "Where were you, Gabrielle?" She wrote a few names on her list, smudging grease on the page.

"I was walking."

"At this hour?" The woman laughed. "Take a little advice from me, *mon petit canard*. Elegant ladies do not go walking all over the city before noon. Sleep is needed to retain beauty." That was hardly true. A great many of the *noblesse* enjoyed walking at the gardens of the Tuileries this early. Élisabeth only embraced the customs that suited her.

"I will try to remember that." Gabrielle sat, folding her hands. "Are you inviting the English ambassador to your card party?"

Élisabeth scrunched her nose. "*Non, merci*. Why would I want a dull ambassador at my card party?"

Gabrielle gnawed on the inside of her cheek. The ambassador was far from dull. He was kind and generous, unlike so many in Society. How could she push back without angering Élisabeth? "He is well liked by many in Paris."

"I am well liked by many in Paris," Élisabeth said, brushing crumbs from her list. "He is tolerated."

"Hardly," Madame de Vintimille said. "He is a favorite of the *dauphine*."

Gabrielle glanced at her stepmother's cousin, but the woman spared her no attention. She wasn't trying to help Gabrielle, that was certain. She simply didn't want a terrible gathering.

"Marie Antoinette is practically still a child." Élisabeth sniffed. "She's younger than Gabrielle. Why would anyone trust her judgment of character?"

"Intelligent or not, she has a great influence at court, and it would be in your favor to invite Lord Stormont." Madame de Vintimilles leaned back in her chair, crossing her arms.

"Will you invite his staff?" Gabrielle asked. "You will want young men to make up your card tables."

"I want young men, yes, but not clerks." Élisabeth reluctantly wrote the ambassador's name on her list.

Gabrielle took a fortifying breath. "I hear the ambassador is hosting a handsome lieutenant just now." If he had an invitation, it would be easier to also invite Monsieur Finch. She could accomplish two things at once.

Élisabeth perked up. "That is better than a clerk."

The thought of Élisabeth flirting with Lieutenant Barlow made Gabrielle bristle. The lieutenant was too compassionate for her. Too genuine. Of course, Gabrielle had only known him for a few hours. Spending more time with him Friday evening would give her a better read of his character.

"I will add him to the list." The quill scratched the paper.

Some of the tension in Gabrielle's shoulders eased. There, an opportunity to introduce the lieutenant to the family, though she didn't know why he would want to know them. She would be more than happy to drop the acquaintance with her stepmother's family entirely.

"*Que diable!*" Her stepmother shot to her feet. "The fitting! We are terribly late."

"I told you that," Madame de Vintimille grumbled.

"Make haste, Gabrielle," her stepmother said through a mouthful of roll. She clapped her hands as Gabrielle stood. "Just think! After this gown is finished, you may have my orange sacque. I do love to help you. Isn't it wonderful that we are so near the same size and you may have all my old gowns?"

Élisabeth hadn't been saying that a moment ago. It was impossible for Gabrielle to forget the *generosity* when so many of her own gowns had been sold and she was left with her stepmother's old ones. While they were of similar height, Élisabeth's gowns did not hit Gabrielle at the right points to make them flattering since Gabrielle was longer through the torso. Still, she nodded.

"What am I not hearing?" Élisabeth inclined her ear dramatically in Gabrielle's direction.

"*Merci*." If only she felt any sort of gratitude toward this woman. More than that, if only she could say what she actually wanted to—that her stepmother had never truly helped her in the seven years since her father's remarriage.

"That's better. Now, hurry and get ready. We depart at any moment." She popped the rest of the roll into her mouth and whisked toward the foyer. "*Au revoir*, Agathe. I will see you soon."

Gabrielle followed her, though because she hadn't even taken off her cloak, she had nothing left to prepare. Élisabeth was the one who wasn't ready. Gabrielle would wait, as she always did, and relish in this little victory she'd won without her stepmother's notice. She had invitations for the ambassador and Lieutenant Barlow. The card party would not be as unbearable this year. She didn't always have so many happy things to look forward to.

Memory of the morning flitted across her consciousness. The bright, happy hues of the *pâtisserie*. The sweetness of the conversation and the food. The warmth that seemed to radiate from the British lieutenant. He'd somehow pulled out admissions she'd tried to keep locked away from the world, and yet his easy smile had given her every reason to trust him.

For the first time in years, someone wanted to help her. She pressed a fist to her lips. Did he know what precious gift he would be giving her if they succeeded in making this match? It might be an amusement to him, a way to pass the time, but it meant freedom to her. She could never repay him. Perhaps there were some good people still left on this earth. And in England, of all the unlikely places.

Harvey set down his quill and scanned what he'd already written in his letter to Admiral Pratt. The man's letter had beat him to Paris, and Harvey couldn't quite fix on why the sight of the missive had filled him with dread. The admiral was to be his father-in-law, after all. He knew the inner workings of the navy, had a keen mind in social and battle settings, and had been gracious in their discussions of the marriage contract so far. There was no reason for this hesitancy.

And yet, as Harvey surveyed the two measly lines he'd managed to write in reply over the last half hour, he had to admit that something clearly gave him pause. Perhaps it wasn't the admiral who was at fault. It very well could be Harvey's father's advice on love and marriage.

"Lost in your correspondence, Barlow?" Lord Stormont stood at the window of the large study, a knowing smile on his face. "A young lady?"

Harvey chuckled to avoid reddening. "No, no, no." Miss Pratt didn't have time for letters. Not to him, anyhow. She much preferred talking to people in the flesh.

Marriage is a business, Harvey. Keep your heart out of it, like I have, and you'll be the wealthiest man on earth.

His father's words rang in his head, as loud as the day he'd first heard them. He'd never admit to anyone how much the words crushed him. Not only had they made him question every hope, but they'd opened his eyes. For the first time he comprehended his mother's guarded looks and the disappointment that peeked out through the creases around her eyes and set of her mouth. She wanted to be appreciated—to be loved—by this man who held so much importance in her life. But she was nothing more than a task on his schedule. Something to be used only when needed. No wonder she'd gone to her sister's under the guise of visiting briefly a few years ago and had never returned to his father's house. With only two sons at sea and far from settled, and the rest of the seventeen being stepchildren, she had few people to rely on. Harvey hoped someday he could change that, though for now she seemed happy where she was.

Harvey cleared his throat, but before he could change

the subject, another thought battered against his mind. Was he putting himself in the same situation with Miss Pratt? Neither of them had feelings for each other, good or bad. She was mildly intrigued by the prospect of prize money and he hoped the connection would help him clear the last obstacles to becoming post-captain.

"I've seen that look before," Lord Stormont said. "It usually relates to a woman."

Harvey sighed. He came to Paris hoping to escape his worries over the union. He did not want to bring this up now.

"Of course you do not have to speak with me about it. But should you wish to discuss it with someone, know that I am a willing confidant." The ambassador said it with friendliness and compassion, a tone so different from Harvey's father when he'd broached the subject. His father had been distracted making an entry in a ledger as they'd discussed. Listening was not his specialty.

"In truth, you are not far off," Harvey finally said.

Stormont nodded. "I knew it was something of that sort. Though I must say, you do not look so distracted as Finch does when poring over his correspondence. Is something wrong?"

Distracted? Harvey's stomach lurched. Was Finch already courting? "I did not know Finch had romantic intentions toward someone."

The ambassador snorted. "Finch gets lovesick over dinner invitations. If he fancies anyone, it passes too quickly for him to act on it. Unfortunately for him, he is oblivious to the ladies who do show him any interest."

"I see." The fact that he didn't have his sights set on a specific young lady should have reassured Harvey that Mademoiselle d'Amilly's quest was not in vain, but if Finch was as fickle as Stormont implied, would she be wasting her time? "Quite the romantic."

"You should hear him reciting Donne." Stormont leaned against the wall next to the window, gazing out into the street. "Someday, someone will catch his eye and he'll realize she returns his affections. One would hope before his heart is broken irreparably. Or hers is."

Harvey had just the girl. Contrary to his recent fear, perhaps this would be easier than he imagined. "If he left his heart out of the equation, he wouldn't get it broken." Gracious, he sounded like his father.

The ambassador turned from the window and fixed Harvey with a thoughtful stare. If Harvey recalled correctly, he wasn't yet fifty, but the man had aged since their last meeting. It wasn't so much the appearance of wrinkles. Rather a deepening of understanding and a slowing of reaction, as though he considered his words more thoroughly before speaking.

"That doesn't sound like the Lieutenant Barlow who visited me in Vienna."

Harvey winced. "I hope I am a bit more wise than that." That was before he'd gone to his father questioning this match with Miss Pratt. Of course his father had pointed out the prudence of such a connection, marrying a girl with a sizable dowry when he was currently on a modest income. A part of him had hoped his father would oppose it so he would have a good excuse not to carry it out.

"You can find a love match and still be wise." Stormont's lips curled. "At least I like to think I had not completely lost my mind when I wed my Henrietta."

"Of course it does happen," Harvey said quickly. But how rare it was. Few people married for love among the aristocracy or the gentry. Even fewer did fifteen years ago.

Those who did, he'd come to observe, were generally the subject of gossip and raised brows for quite some time afterward. He'd seen it first hand with the few of his brothers and sisters who married for love. "Most of us don't have the time or resources to wait for such a match."

Stormont nodded. "There may be truth in that." He found his way to a chair across the desk from Harvey. "Are you engaged, Lieutenant?"

"I expect to soon be." Harvey retrieved his pen and dipped it in the inkwell. This blasted letter needed to be written.

"You sound rather *enthusiastic* about the prospect."

"I simply do not know her well." He hoped future interactions gave him more cause to anticipate the union. Perhaps they could establish some form of friendship before.

The ambassador crossed his ankle over his knee and leaned back in the chair, studying Harvey. "Henrietta has been gone these eight years."

Had it already been eight? Harvey paused his twiddling of the quill.

"I perhaps might have avoided heartache if I'd indifferently married some English girl picked by my parents rather than a Viennese beauty. But I don't regret it for a moment."

Harvey said nothing. Why was Stormont telling him this?

"Don't rule out a love match just because your father couldn't be bothered with love. The easiest course does not usually lead to the greatest treasure."

Harvey tried not to squirm under the ambassador's fierce stare. He looked away quickly, setting down his pen. Time to strike his colors and try again with this missive later when his unease over the marriage discussions wouldn't be called to the forefront of his mind.

"This is a stunning desk," he said, running a hand over the gilded decor along the sides.

Stormont relaxed. "It's a Riesener. He built it to commemorate the marriage of the *dauphin* and *dauphine*. The *dauphine* gave it to me when I arrived, in gratitude for the friendship we established back in Vienna when she was a girl. Shocking what a little kindness can mean to someone."

Shocking indeed. The remembrance of Mademoiselle d'Amilly's hesitant smile as she slowly extended her trust bloomed in his mind. Perhaps this mission would be more than just a diplomatic assignment. In the midst of his uncertain future, this could be the warmth he sought.

"Do you know Mademoiselle d'Amilly?" Harvey asked, pushing back from the desk.

A laughing twinkle hit the ambassador's eye. "Gabrielle d'Amilly? I've met her, yes. Lovely young lady."

"Madame Necker has extended her an invitation to Friday evening's gathering. Might we offer to escort her to the event?"

The ambassador straightened. "Oh, yes. Of course. I will send a message to the Hôtel d'Hallwyll."

"Excellent." It would be more time with Finch with fewer people about. And more time for Harvey to ascertain the situation. He stood, swiping the unfinished letter and pen into his writing box, then capping the ink. This young Frenchwoman who wanted to get away so badly had intrigued him. She might prove the distraction he needed to resettle his head in order to return to England with a clearer vision of the right path forward.

CHAPTER 5

Élisabeth sighed theatrically as she paused on the doorstep. "Are you certain you will not join us to dine with the Family Saint-Jacques? They have a son, you know. A rich one."

Gabrielle clasped her hands behind her. The son was about as rich as Élisabeth according to rumors, borrowing money and adding up debts without thought. "I promised Madame Necker."

"Yes, yes." Élisabeth tapped her petticoat with her fan. "Only next time, you must try to get an invitation to a different salon. Madame Geoffrin or someone a little more civilized than the Neckers. He's just a banker, you know."

And Père was an untitled small landowner until Élisabeth got her hands on him and his business. A farmer who rented the same house the Neckers used to inhabit.

Her stepmother pouted. "I will practically be by myself with all those people."

Gabrielle closed her eyes. *Lord, give me strength.* "Your mother is going with you."

"How could you do that to me?" Élisabeth sauntered

back into the house, and Gabrielle tensed. She'd almost been free. "You've never gone off on your own like this before."

"I'm not on my own," Gabrielle said. "I'll be escorted by—"

"A troop of Englishmen!" she said. Behind Élisabeth, the footman stood with the door half closed as though unsure if he should shut it until she was done and wished to leave or keep it open until she made up her mind. "You would desert me for our enemies! It's rather heartless, do you not think?"

It wasn't heartless at all. Gabrielle refrained from kneading her brow against the beginnings of a headache. "Élisabeth, we haven't been at war with England for several years."

"Is that so?" She gave Gabrielle a bewildered look. "How very strange. We're usually at war with them."

"Thank you for your concern," she said carefully. "I really will be all right. And tonight you may tell me all about the inferior menu of Madame Saint-Jacques."

Élisabeth's face brightened. "I suppose it will have to do. I know you will be waiting anxiously to hear. But you must overcome this obsession with the English. First the card party, and now this. It is quite distressing."

Gabrielle smiled wanly. She'd subtracted time from this moment and added it to after the salon meeting when Élisabeth would lecture her mercilessly, but it would be worth it to not have her stepmother on the threshold when the party of Englishmen arrived.

Her stepmother snatched her hand and pulled her in to plant a large kiss on each cheek, and Gabrielle prayed the rouge from Élisabeth's lips could easily be blended in. "*Petite bête*. What a silly girl you are. Go dine with your pompous *philosophes* and that mouse of a woman. Someday you'll learn there are more important people to give your consideration." She turned on her heel and swept out the door, the young footman barely getting the door open in time.

When he closed it, the footman sighed. Then he reddened and glanced in Gabrielle's direction, eyes wide with concern.

She gave her own big sigh and a small smile to try to put him at ease. "A few hours' reprieve when we've both gone."

He nodded, grinning. "You will be leaving soon as well, *non*?"

"Any moment, I expect."

"Should you not be above?" the young man asked. "I thought grand ladies descended from their *toilette* rather than waiting in the vestibule."

"Oh." She was not a grand lady, but he had a point. It wouldn't do to be standing at the door as though desperate to leave. "I think you must be correct." She turned quickly, gathering her skirts and hurrying up the staircase. Surely Finch would come retrieve her. She wanted to make an impression. Preferably a good one. She darted around the corner at the top of the stairs and leaned against the wall, waiting for a knock. She fiddled with a curl, then stopped herself at the thought of getting hair powder on her gown. The maid had needed to use a brown powder because her more fashionable white powder was mysteriously missing. Élisabeth must have borrowed it.

Gabrielle absently brushed at her shoulders to clear off any stray powder. When the door opened, she would wait for a few moments, then glide over to the top of the staircase and pause. Yes, that seemed right. And then she would descend slowly with a touch of eagerness. But not too much eagerness. She didn't want to frighten him away.

A confident rap on the door sent a thrill down her spine. She straightened and tried to smooth the front of the bright orange sacque gown Élisabeth had given her. The waist was too high on her, making the side pleats of the gown hang oddly over her paniers, but it couldn't be helped. She'd tried tying the paniers higher up, but they wouldn't stay. And then there was the neckline. *Bonté divine*. It gapped horribly from improper pinning. The door opened, but she couldn't make out the strong voice's greeting as she unpinned and then re-pinned the bodice. There. That should do it.

She scrambled out to the top of the stairs, catching her shoe on the rug and nearly turning her ankle in her haste. *Poise, Gabrielle*. She righted herself and turned toward the stairs. Demure smile, sweep of her slightly too-short skirts, and meet his eye.

Except it wasn't Monsieur Finch's dark eyes she met. Lieutenant Barlow slowly removed his hat, gaze fixed on her. His face softened and a light grin played across his lips. His hair was simply dressed and only lightly powdered so that his natural dark-honey color peeked through. His coat, a much more elegant version of the one he wore on their first meeting, seemed almost bright blue in the light of the vestibule, his gold buttons gleaming. The fine wool hugged the lines of his shoulders in a way that emphasized their sturdiness. It was the sort of image she might stop and stare at for hours if hung in a gallery.

And here she was standing at the top of the stairs gawking in a dress that fit her all wrong. Gabrielle hurried down the stairs, gripping the handrail to avoid tripping again. Where was Monsieur Finch? Somehow she felt more comfortable at the thought of standing next to him. He was not quite so well put-together.

"Mademoiselle." Even his bow was graceful and not overly self-important. "Are you ready?"

"*Bonsoir*, Lieutenant." She curtsied quickly, tugging at her gown once more. It was a good thing she didn't have intentions toward this Englishman. "I think—"

The distinct click of a pin on tile halted the words in her throat. A quick glance down showed the front edge of one side of her gown, which was supposed to overlap her stomacher, lying limp and loose over her chest. *Ciel!* She slapped a hand across the unfastened opening and searched the floor, face flaming. "These stupid gowns," she muttered. "None of them fit." The pin had probably dropped into the grout between the tiles, impossible to locate. She turned away from the lieutenant. Thank heavens it wasn't Monsieur Finch. How many times would she make a fool of herself in front of Lieutenant Barlow? She needed to run upstairs whether she found the cursed pin or not.

The footman gave her a grimace of pity and hurried from the vestibule. She hoped in search of another pin.

"Mademoiselle."

She swallowed and turned around, unable to help the humiliation that scrunched her face. Lieutenant Barlow held up the traitorous pin.

"I cannot help but think that perhaps you are not entirely comfortable in the gown you are wearing."

Gabrielle's shoulders sagged of their own accord. She couldn't deny it. "Most of my clothes were my stepmother's. We are almost the same size, but she's more..." What was she doing? She couldn't talk to him about *that*. She cleared her throat. "My stepmother just isn't quite the same and hasn't bothered to have the gowns altered to better fit."

She hadn't dared to try fixing them herself for fear that Élisabeth would get angry for ruining her gowns.

His brows pulled together. "You've nothing better suited?"

There was the blue gown Père had given her. The one she'd begged him for and he'd finally bought her, much to Élisabeth's frustration. But Élisabeth's arguments hadn't held much sway that year, not with the flurry of rumors surrounding her and Père's increasing dismay. Her stepmother's reputation had worked in Gabrielle's favor for once.

"I have one made to fit me, but it is a few years old."

Lieutenant Barlow smiled kindly. "That should not matter."

Gabrielle inched toward the stairs, still holding her gown closed. "I shall keep you all waiting."

He motioned toward the street. "Finch and Stormont fell asleep in the coach on our way here. You have a few moments."

Asleep? With this mishap, that was fortunate. "You don't mind waiting?" she asked.

"Not at all." He winked, waving her upstairs.

What a considerate and sympathetic man. Gabrielle dashed up the stairs, spirits lifting despite her embarrassing debacle. What could have been a terrible omen had somehow righted itself and she could only hope it lasted through the evening.

When Mademoiselle d'Amilly returned to the top of the stairs, Harvey blinked. She floated down, the pale blue silk of her petticoat whispering against the rungs of the banister. The gown was an older style of *robe á l'anglaise*—appropriate, since she was trying to catch an Englishman with an English style gown—which fit neatly at her waist to emphasize her willowy figure.

"Ah, yes. This will do nicely," he said when she reached the bottom of the stairs. He extended his hand to her, and she took it delicately. "It suits you much better than your stepmother's gown. In fit and color."

Something strange overtook him, and he gripped her hand, suddenly spinning her around to display the change of clothing. She gave a little yelp, but it turned into a laugh by the time she made it back around from her twirl. Her skirts swished about her and her cheeks pinked.

"I was not ready for that." A lively light touched her eyes, which had a hint of azure in their green depths drawn out by the color of her gown.

Harvey nodded once. "Finch will hardly be able to take his eyes off you." Likewise all the other men at the dinner. Would Madame Necker approve of such a distraction in her salon? One couldn't predict the level of distraction with men like Morellet and Marmontel. One day these *philosophes* could throw themselves so intensely into their debates so as not to be disturbed by anything, and the next be diverted by the mere mention of a pretty face.

"Monsieur Finch won't mind it's not the latest style?" She squeezed his hand a little tighter.

"Of course he won't." He pulled her toward the door, and the footman hurried to open it, a pin in one hand and confused look on his face. If Harvey had anything to do with it, Finch would be the most distracted of them all this evening.

"You are too kind, Lieutenant." The way she addressed

him—a very French LYOO-ten-awn—sent a little spark of warmth through his chest. What an odd sensation. It wasn't one he'd felt in quite some time.

Harvey halted before exiting the house. He turned to her. "Perhaps we should discuss our plan for this evening."

"Our plan?"

He glanced at the carriage. Finch's head was still pressed against the window, lopsided. Asleep. They had a moment to spare.

"We are attempting to get you as much time with Finch as possible, but that is a little difficult in such a group. You must stay at his side any moment you can while we aren't at the table."

She tilted her head. "That won't seem terribly obvious?"

"Well, you mustn't make it awkward. We have to walk that fine line between not catching his eye and repelling him with too much forwardness."

Her lips twisted. "I do not know if I am capable of that. As we've seen in our few meetings, I am practically a master of awkwardness."

She wasn't entirely wrong on that count. He gulped back a chuckle. "Positivity, mademoiselle, or we will never reach our goal."

"I will attempt to remain in his company as long as I can manage." The young woman straightened solemnly, as though she'd resolved to complete a perilous act of espionage. "Was there anything else?"

Still no movement in the carriage. Afternoon light glinted off the ambassador's livery on the sides of the vehicle. "How well informed are you on Parisian architecture?" he asked.

"I know little more than that it livens our streets."

"Perhaps we may find a book seller and secure a volume on the subject."

"Architecture?" Her brows knit.

"What is so terrible about that? Do you not read?"

She pressed her lips together. "Of course I read. More people in my country can read than in yours. However, I did not think I would be returning to the school room in pursuit of this gentleman."

"One must be a life-long learner to achieve their goals. You have to keep Finch's attention with something until he's caught."

She sighed, then nodded. "I am not very good at this."

He offered her his arm. They didn't want to be too late to the Neckers'. "It is fortunate you do not have to do it alone, then."

Her arm slid hesitantly around his, long fingers resting on the blue wool of his sleeve. "Have you had much experience helping to make matches?"

He led her through the door and down the steps. The rue Michel le Compte was quickly filling with coaches carting the wealthy off to various dinner parties. "With seventeen older brothers and sisters, I've played my part in a few schemes."

Mademoiselle d'Amilly pulled on his arm. "Seventeen?" Her eyes grew large as carriage wheels.

"My father has been married several times," he said quickly, but the shock didn't leave her face. "You should see all the grandchildren."

She gave a nervous laugh as though her mind couldn't quite wrap around the idea of so many people.

A footman hopped down from the coach as they approached.

"Do you have many brothers and sisters, mademoiselle?" Harvey asked as they waited for him to open the door.

"Not one."

It was fortunate, then, that she had her sights set on Finch, though he couldn't help feeling sorry for her. She seemed quite alone and not in a good way. With a sister she might have had someone with whom to commiserate, and with a brother she wouldn't have needed the help of a near stranger to attempt this match.

"I have secured invitations to the card party," she said quietly.

"Excellent." Holding up her end of the bargain. He should have guessed she would be quick about it.

The ambassador and the secretary startled awake as Harvey handed Mademoiselle d'Amilly into the coach and climbed in himself. She settled next to Finch, who drew out a pleasant smile as he greeted her. She blushed faintly and threw Harvey a grateful look before giving her full attention to Finch.

Something stirred in the corners of Harvey's heart, a warmth and anticipation he hadn't known for some time. She was an attractive young woman despite her stepmother's gowns, but sitting across from him at ease in a gown made for her, he had to admit she was more than simply attractive. The soft blue contrasted with her rich brown curls in a manner that made it difficult to pull his eyes away.

"Something on your mind, Barlow?" Lord Stormont asked.

Harvey laughed. Only that Finch was an incredibly lucky man.

CHAPTER 6

Gabrielle's visions of an enchanted evening fizzled before they'd finished their soup. She'd done as Lieutenant Barlow instructed, staying close to Monsieur Finch as they waited to go in to dinner and hanging onto his every word through the meal, but Monsieur Finch paid her no more attention than he did to Madame Necker or Madame d'Épinay. He'd taken to telling stories about himself that few of their company listened to.

"And that is why I say most enthusiastically that one must always bring a spare pair of shoes when walking in English fields, no matter how quaint they appear," Monsieur Finch said with a chuckle. "Cow-sharn is not a welcome companion." He returned to cutting into his fish.

Gabrielle forced the corners of her mouth upward, not quite following the Englishman's joke. Cow...sharn? Is that what he'd said? It must have been an English word mixed in with his French. Either he was speaking of the need to avoid mud in the field or something rather unsavory for a dinner conversation. She snatched up her drink, hoping he wouldn't notice her confusion. Why was Monsieur Finch traipsing through fields? She knew he wasn't particularly wealthy, but surely England had roads. *Dommage*, her cheeks were hurting from trying to laugh at all these jokes she couldn't understand.

Across from them, the ambassador and Lieutenant Barlow exchanged a glance. The lieutenant's eyes creased at the corners as though he'd taken a sip of scalding chocolate. The ambassador held a napkin to his face, but he couldn't disguise his barely-held-in laughter. Gabrielle got the feeling he was not laughing at Monsieur Finch's joke so much as the situation.

She dropped her gaze to the carp with blue sauce on her plate. It was cooked in a lovely manner but carried the same satisfaction as this bland conversation. She eyed the Neckers and the *philosophes* who weren't religious with their plates full of rich beef. What a shame that it was Friday and Lent. If only she could find a way to unlock rich conversation, having been deprived of the meat.

Lieutenant Barlow shifted, causing the gold trim of his dress uniform to glint in the candlelight. He wasn't as extravagantly dressed as some of their company, but he seemed to draw the attention of the room with ease. Was it the naturally warm timbre of his voice that pulled them in or the way his eyes seemed to smile even when his lips were not?

"Madame d'Épinay, would you be so good as to tell us more about your book?" he asked. "Mademoiselle d'Amilly and I were discussing what an accomplishment it is to create a work of literature. She was especially eager to learn more."

The middle-aged woman turned a self-satisfied look on Gabrielle. What was the lieutenant doing? Eyes around the table focused on her. Including Finch's, which held what she hoped was a mildly intrigued expression. So that was it. If she couldn't get Finch to pay her the attention she needed on his own, the lieutenant would force him to regard her.

She swallowed the dryness in her mouth before she spoke. "I found the concept of a conversation between mother and daughter rather sweet." It was true. If only she'd had that in her own life as she grew. If only she had that now. She wouldn't be relying on a near stranger for help.

"Women's stories are always sweet," muttered Monsieur d'Alembert. The *philosophe*, who lived on the same street as Gabrielle, had the usual cold disposition she'd noticed on the few occasions they'd met before. He said the word sweet as though tasting a rotten fruit. Gabrielle ground her teeth. She shouldn't say anything. She should just let the *philosophe* have his grumpy aside and ignore it.

"That should not lessen their value," she blurted before she had time to rein in her thoughts. "Sweet things have an important place in our world. Likewise, so do women."

The table quieted but not in anticipation as it had before. She, a girl of three-and-twenty at her very first dinner at Madame Necker's salon, had contradicted a *philosophe* of the fame and prowess of d'Alembert. Heat drained from her face. She couldn't read the hostess's careful expression at the head of the table. This would be her first and only attendance at this salon.

She might as well finish if she had nothing to lose. "Women have as much right, as much duty, to learn as anyone, which I am led to believe is the subject of Madame d'Épinay's book. How can a truly enlightened society be achieved if half her citizenry is not supported in expanding their minds to reach their full potential?" Gabrielle realized she was gripping her fork like a weapon and lowered it to her plate with great effort.

"I, of course, mean no offense to our guest of honor, our distinguished authoress, when I say this," d'Alembert said, "but I think it fitting that she keeps her discourse to conversations between women and girls in the home where they belong. Even Rousseau does not think educating a woman worth the hassle, as it gives women ideas that they should be at the forefront of Society rather than supporters of it."

Gabrielle attacked her fish with all the fervor she had left. He could keep his dogmatic ideas. She would not try to dissuade an obstinately ignorant fool. What a mess she'd made of the conversation. Lieutenant Barlow had presented her an opportunity, and she'd squandered it. Neither of the other ladies at the table had felt a need to put the *philosophe* in his place.

A soft snort, almost imperceptible, sounded from down the table. Madame d'Épinay took up her glass and spoke into the crimson liquid. "Rousseau is a *crétin*." Harsh words to utter in a gathering of his peers. She gave Gabrielle a sly look of approval, which only half lifted her spirits. Madame d'Épinay may not fault her for standing her ground, but Madame Necker gave no hint whether she agreed or resented the argument Gabrielle had sparked.

The Englishmen had remained quiet through the exchanges, but Monsieur Finch finally entered the fray with a cheerful, "I would be perfectly happy with a pleasant and unaffected wife, well-educated or otherwise."

Gabrielle's heart sank. Pleasant. Unaffected. She hardly considered herself either of those.

"You see?" Another of the *philosophes*, a former abbot by the name of Raynal, said. "Even the English can agree that more important in a woman's development is learning to play the part of a keeper of the home. Not her education or her reason."

The *philosophes* did not seem keen to let the matter drop. Gabrielle sank back into her chair. It was barely evening, but she wanted the night to be over. Madame Necker was known for her disapproval of heated arguments and anyone who incited them, and while it had yet to get terribly heated, an edge had crept into the men's voices. All this and she'd gained no ground with Monsieur Finch.

"You admit that women have reason," Madame d'Épinay said as a footman appeared at her side to take her empty plate. "And yet you wish us to do nothing with it."

"Perhaps one could make such an argument," l'Abbé Raynal said, glancing across the table to d'Alembert.

The severe *philosophe* answered, "Yes, I admit that women have some reason, even if it is most often ill used."

"Miss Mary Astell made a fantastic point in her work," came the soothing voice of Lieutenant Barlow. It flowed through Gabrielle's soul like warm honey. He didn't look at her, but somehow it felt as though he were speaking just to her rather than a table of well-respected and learned men. "Are you familiar with Miss Astell?"

"If she is English, I think not," l'Abbé Raynal said.

"A pity, because she had many fascinating things to say," the lieutenant said. "A woman ahead of her time. She said..." He paused, staring at the ceiling as though deep in thought. Perhaps translating the phrase into French in his mind. "'If God had not intended that women should use their reason, He would not have given them any, for He does nothing in vain.'" His eyes met Gabrielle's, and he gave her an encouraging smile.

A jumble of thoughts and feelings erupted in Gabrielle's

mind all at once. The lieutenant believed in her, and not just in her abilities to secure a match with Monsieur Finch. He believed in her as a rational human being, unlike the *philosophes* sitting near them. The respect that radiated from his gaze set her heart alight. In their short acquaintance he might have mocked her for the ridiculous things she'd said or done. Instead he'd seen her plight and offered her help. It was a shame he was not staying in Paris longer, or she might consider switching her target.

"My cook has made a special treat for us this evening," Madame Necker said as a large plate of tartelettes was placed on the table. Thin strips of pastry crisscrossed the top of each. "We have named them *tartes conversations* after our dear friend's book, *Conversations d'Émilie*."

Emboldened by the lieutenant's silent affirmation, Gabrielle turned to Monsieur Finch and offered him a genial smile. "How delicious. Do you enjoy pastries, monsieur? Have you a favorite?"

Monsieur Finch laughed as he took the serving utensil and slid one of the tartelettes onto her plate before serving himself. "Not like Lieutenant Barlow. I do like something sweet once in a while." He turned to offer one to Madame d'Épinay without answering her other question.

Why couldn't this be easy? She plucked up her fork again. Monsieur Finch hadn't seemed like a difficult man to catch when she settled on him. She'd just have to keep trying.

Gabrielle cut a small bite of the tart and brought it to her mouth. Crisp icing, sweet and soft almond cream, and buttery pastry. The lieutenant gave a small sigh, his well-formed shoulders relaxing as he chewed his first bite. The tension that had coiled up inside her since the beginning of dinner slowly unwound at the sight of his simple pleasure in the treat. Perhaps the mistake at the gardens of the Tuileries was not so much a misfortune as it was a stroke of good luck. The sort of good luck she hadn't had for quite some time. To practically fall into the acquaintance of a gentleman so capable and kind was something she wouldn't have imagined just a week ago. After all the heaviness of trying to determine what to do on her own, how comforting it was to have someone who cared about her future, even if he knew her but little. She took another bite, allowing herself to embrace the lieutenant's joy.

With his help, she would succeed. She had to believe it.

Harvey leaned against the wall near the salon's extensive bookshelf, a cup of coffee that had been brewed far too long in one hand. Across the room, Mademoiselle d'Amilly sat on a sofa beside Finch hanging onto his every word.

Finch was as dense as a fog bank. Harvey scrubbed a hand over his face. Any other man in the room would have been flattered by the young lady's attention. Madame Necker and Madame d'Épinay had already exchanged a knowing look over the marked preference being paid. The clerk seemed absolutely oblivious.

She would have to catch his attention a little more drastically. And with more regularity. Harvey only had a few weeks to help her, and she needed to have Finch half in love with her by the time he left.

"Did the Admiralty send you to spy on our young women, Lieutenant?"

Harvey blinked as Raynal appeared at his side,

searching the bookshelves. Most of the volumes were dressed in fine green leather and titled in gold lettering.

"I beg pardon, but I do not understand," Harvey said, straightening and taking a sip of the coffee. It was all he could do to prevent his face from scrunching at the bitterness. He should have asked for more sugar.

"*Vous reluquez notre petite invitée.*"

Reluquez? That word was unfamiliar. He furrowed his brow. No words came to mind. *Notre petite invitée*. Our little guest. Mademoiselle d'Amilly? She was by far the youngest of the gathering.

"*Vous la regardiez.*" The former abbot leaned in. "*Longuement.*"

You were regarding her for a long time. Harvey closed his eyes. The man was accusing him of staring at Mademoiselle d'Amilly. He couldn't admit the truth, but if someone thought he was the one pursuing the young lady, it could undermine their efforts.

"Perhaps you fancy taking home a memento of Paris?" the abbot asked.

"I don't plan to take anything back with me," Harvey said coolly. Anything except the observations he'd been sent to obtain. "Or anyone."

"What a pity. She is a handsome girl."

That she was. And besides a couple of enquiring looks in his direction, she'd been a vision of confidence since dinner finished. The simplicity of her hair and gown let her natural beauty shine rather than distracting from it like her stepmother's gowns did.

Finch said something, and Mademoiselle d'Amilly laughed. A genuine laugh this time, like the one Harvey had pulled from her at the *pâtisserie*. He registered a hint of relief. She'd been forcing laughs all evening. Finch finally figured out how to say something amusing. Well done.

"Very handsome. And bright as well. She will make someone a fine and intelligent wife someday." He couldn't help taking a shot over the *philosophes*' pompous rhetoric from the dinner conversation.

"Then you had better take advantage of the peace time, Lieutenant," the abbot said. "And who knows how long the peace will last? *Dieu seul le sait.*"

Perhaps God only knew the exact amount of time peace would last, but there were a multitude of hypotheses through the Admiralty and Parliament. "Why would France start a war now? England certainly wouldn't."

He'd speak with confidence and let the *philosophe* tell him he was wrong. An intellectual could not help himself when it came to correcting seemingly erroneous statements. Few more willingly spilled information than an intellectual righting a perceived error of rationality. They were nearly as bad as those who fancied themselves knowledgeable about the happenings of the court.

"Yes, you seem to have your hands full with the Americans." A smug smile pulled at Raynal's mouth.

Harvey shrugged, though he felt far from calm on the subject. Naval officers cheered the outbreak of war and its reprieve from the dullness and scarcity of half pay ashore. Harvey yearned for the prestige of commanding his own ship and having everything ordered just as he wished. He loved the thrill of hunting down an enemy and taking a prize. But ever looming in Harvey's mind were the casualties. War came at a hefty price, and not just for the nations' pocketbooks. "We'll reconcile with the colonies soon enough. They haven't the sources nor the unity to oppose Great Britain for long."

Raynal harrumphed. "I said it five years ago and believe it still. England's hold on America is in its final throes. The age of the enlightened man—the man who can think for himself and control his own destiny free from the chains of monarchy—has arrived."

Mademoiselle d'Amilly's slender fingers played with one of her curls as she hung onto every word Finch said, whether to her or to Madame d'Épinay. He could almost see the gears in her mind spinning like a newly wound clock as she tried to find a place to say something witty or flattering. "The age of the enlightened man," Harvey said thoughtfully. "But not the enlightened woman."

"*Quel charmeur*," Raynal remarked. "It is a wonder you haven't secured a wife, being such a defender of the weaker sex."

"I will be engaged practically the moment I set foot on English soil." The image of Miss Pratt's lofty smile hit his consciousness with such force his breath caught. Not from her beauty, but from the casual indifference in her blue eyes.

Raynal nodded thoughtfully. "*Tous mes voeux*, Lieutenant. You will make a fine husband."

And a fine captain, he hoped.

"As you said, I must take advantage of the peace." Harvey took another bitter sip and tried not to wince. "If the colonies revolt, as you think they will, what is to keep revolution from spilling to all colonies throughout the world? Or even to Europe? Think of the devastation."

The abbot frowned. "France would do well to restrict access to foreigners for this reason. Present company excluded, of course."

Harvey didn't believe him. The abbot was notorious for disliking foreigners, friend or foe.

"However," the man said as he adjusted his wig, "perhaps the time has come for change to show its face. To put off the shackles of our history and embrace a different and brighter future."

It didn't come as a surprise that a *philosophe*, one of the intellectual elite of Paris, was in support of the colonists. He'd assumed most were before he came to France. One confirmation secured. Now what of people such as the Neckers, those of wealth earned in trade? What of the *noblesse*? He could only hope Mademoiselle d'Amilly's connections would prove beneficial in getting him the information Admiral Pratt desired.

As if sensing he was regarding her, the mademoiselle turned to catch his eye. She smiled, one of the genuinely delighted smiles that made a man yearn for quiet evenings at home in front of a small fire, a plate piled with pastries on the tea cart, and conversation with her alone. That could never be for him, however. Whenever relations dissolved with the colonists, he'd be off across the Atlantic. It was fortunate, then, that Miss Pratt was his destiny, a woman who would hardly notice he was gone. Mademoiselle d'Amilly deserved a man at her side, and he would do all he could in the next few weeks to ensure that happened. He sincerely hoped that Finch was worthy of her.

CHAPTER 7

Nearly a week after the only mildly successful dinner at Madame Necker's, Gabrielle awoke to find a note on a platter beside her bed. Her name and the directions were written in a bold, masculine hand that made her heart skip. She pushed herself up and snatched the square of paper from the table. How had she not woken when the servant brought it in?

She knelt in the warm covers and tore around the wafer seal to open the paper. The evening must have been more successful than she thought for Finch to send something so early in the morning. She unfolded it, a smile already on her face.

Mademoiselle d'Amilly,

You will forgive my boldness in writing at such an hour.

She gave a little laugh. *Naturellement*, there was nothing to forgive.

The ambassador has secured the company of Monsieur Ange-Jacques Gabriel, the king's architect, to show us the Place Louis XV this afternoon.

Ah. Architecture. She'd seen the newly finished square not long ago. It was...stately. He wouldn't risk writing a note simply to tell her about the buildings, would he? Was he asking her to come to the meeting? She tapped her fist against her mouth. Élisabeth hadn't told her of any events today. No fittings or invitations. If he wanted her to come with him, she'd do anything in her power to attend. Hearing from the architect himself should make the afternoon interesting, especially for Monsieur Finch. Perhaps she could glean some facts to use in future conversation.

I have secured the attendance of Madame d'Épinay, who will transport you to the square a little before 2 p.m if you are not otherwise engaged.

She most certainly was not. Gabrielle swung her legs out of bed, hardly noticing the chill air hitting her skin. She hopped to her feet. She'd wear Élisabeth's brown riding habit. It almost fit correctly. The more masculine cut hid the fact it fell limp in front, and the longer skirt made up for her height.

Would Monsieur Finch be in the carriage? Not that it mattered. Lieutenant Barlow said he always slept in coaches, whether the journey was short or long.

Finch told me he would be there.

She halted on her way to the armoire, eyes dropping from her place to the signature.

H. Barlow

Oh. Her shoulders slumped. It wasn't from Monsieur Finch at all. She sighed. This was simply to continue their mission. *Très bien*. She shouldn't hope to gain his favor this quickly. Lieutenant Barlow was not a magician, after all. But word from him was a good thing. She eagerly went back to finish what he'd written.

Unless he forgets that he has agreed to meet the ambassador and me, I expect we shall have a pleasant day with plenty of opportunities to impress. Bring your charm and your lovely smile, and do not spend too long worrying over what to wear. It will be of little importance.

If only she believed that. She glanced once more at the signature, then refolded the note. H. Barlow. She wondered what the H stood for. She dug out her stockings, garters, and shoes and sat in the small chair by her dressing table. As she pulled the stockings on, her mind kept wandering back to Lieutenant Barlow's words. Her charm? He thought her charming? And after only two meetings.

Would that Finch had been so easily convinced of her charm. He was making this game of matchmaking far more difficult than Gabrielle anticipated.

GABRIELLE RUSHED out the door after convincing Élisabeth that Madame d'Épinay, being a woman with friends in high places, was a worthy chaperone. The woman's carriage sat waiting in the cramped street, horses shuffling impatiently. She slid into the seat across from the older woman.

"*Merci*, madame. You are too kind to convey me to the square."

The woman smiled mysteriously. "Anything for our lieutenant."

Really it was for Monsieur Finch, but Gabrielle wouldn't dare correct her. The coach jerked forward before settling into a steady rattle over the uneven streets.

"Will you attend Madame Necker's salon this week?"

she asked. Madame Necker, to her relief, had invited Gabrielle back for a second meeting.

Madame d'Épinay shook her head. "Not this week." She settled back into the plush seat of the coach and leaned her head back. "The publication of a novel is quite draining. One must relax afterward, and some *philosophes* who frequent Madame Necker's salon are rather tiresome. Not to mention her husband." She snorted in a rather unladylike fashion.

Gabrielle cocked her head. "Monsieur Necker has never seemed very tiresome to me." She'd only met him on a couple of occasions. Though he never remembered her, and they had to be re-introduced each time.

"Have you heard the man speak? He only has a mind for numbers and calculations. He cannot make a rational argument about anything else."

Long rows of buildings passed on either side of them, some stately and classical in the more recent style, some old and twisted in the medieval style. She really should learn a thing or two about architecture. Monsieur Finch had brought up the architectural features of the Neckers' house frequently the past Friday evening.

"At least he seems to respect his wife," Gabrielle said.

"That much is true." The woman's eyes showed she had many more thoughts on the subject, but silence prevailed as they made their way toward the palaces of the Louvre and Tuileries.

Columns. Gabrielle knew what those were. Facades. That was an architectural term, was it not? And then there were...doors?

At one point they passed a particularly narrow section of street when the stench became unbearable. Both ladies held handkerchiefs to their noses, and Gabrielle was grateful she'd found the old bottle of honey water to spritz hers with. She hoped London would not smell as wretched as Paris, but she guessed it would be rather similar. Cities were cities.

The gardens of the Tuileries passed to her right, and she couldn't help picking out the spot where she'd met Lieutenant Barlow. How she'd wanted to disappear from embarrassment at the confusion. Now she was seeking out his company regularly. Things had changed so quickly.

"If I may be so bold," Madame d'Épinay said, "I would offer a word of advice."

Gabrielle straightened. "Of course, madame."

The other woman leaned closer. "I am old enough to be your mother, but take this as from a friend who only wishes the best for you and who has learned this lesson the hard way."

There was something ominous about the way she said the last part that made Gabrielle clasp her hands. When Élisabeth gave her advice, it was always with derision, as though her stepmother thought her too stupid to know better. But there was respect and real concern in Madame d'Épinay's eyes, serious as they were.

"Only give your heart to a man who respects you," the madame said. "The men who do not are not worth the heartache they will undoubtedly cause."

Gabrielle nodded slowly. Did Madame d'Épinay sense her aim in securing a match? "How will I know if they respect me?"

The woman took one hand out of her fur muff. "Watch him when you speak," she said, pointing her finger for emphasis. "Does he look like he is simply waiting for a pause in your speaking so he can interject with his own intelligent comment? Or is he hanging on to your every word? Does he seem to genuinely enjoy discussing important things with you, or does he save the topics for drinking with his friends? Is he honest with you?" She sat taller. "Does he praise your looks and not your mind? Is he only concerned about your beauty and how fine you will look on his arm at parties?"

"I don't have to worry about him seeking me out for that," Gabrielle interjected with a nervous laugh. Élisabeth made sure to remind her that men would not be marrying her for beauty.

"Nonsense," Madame d'Épinay said with a wave. "You are certainly at risk. But do not give in unless they have earned it. Even the most intelligent of men are susceptible to being cads." Her mouth twisted, eyes clouding. "Make them earn your respect by respecting you, and then never let them forget the respect you deserve."

"I will try." What a daunting task. Very few people in this world truly respected her.

"You will succeed." Madame d'Épinay patted Gabrielle's knee. "You are an intelligent girl, and there is a fire in you. We saw a little of it at Friday's dinner."

Gabrielle's face heated at the memory of her outburst. "I hope I did not offend."

"Ha! The *philosophes* are used to offense. Each of them is offended at someone every day of the year. Enlightened men always are. They need a regular dose of humility at the hand of a woman. That is why Diderot and Grimm are in Russia; they needed a great dose, and only Catherine could administer it."

A grin split Gabrielle's face at the pun and did not leave

until the carriage stopped and she was handed down by Lieutenant Barlow. He assisted without an air of superiority, looking truly pleased to see her, and for the briefest moment she forgot she wasn't there on purpose to spend time with the lieutenant. In that moment, she wished the threat of war that would take him away, leaving her alone in an unfamiliar country, was not so real a threat. It was easy to imagine loving Lieutenant Barlow.

She blinked. Monsieur Finch. It was also easy to imagine loving Monsieur Finch. Releasing the lieutenant's hand, she moved away quickly so he could assist Madame d'Épinay. She scanned the gathering around the coach. The ambassador, an aide at his side, stood near a rather old gentleman in fine clothing, but there was no sign of Monsieur Finch. He was probably out admiring the buildings.

Lieutenant Barlow offered her his arm, which she took with hesitation. She was supposed to be spending time with Finch, though the lieutenant was not a bad alternative until they found the clerk. She just had to keep her thoughts from straying down paths they were not supposed to go.

"Allow me to introduce you to Monsieur Gabriel," the lieutenant said, guiding her toward the older men. "He has been quite generous with his information about the place already."

"Monsieur Finch will be happy about that." She lowered her voice to a whisper. "Where is Monsieur Finch?"

Lieutenant Barlow winced. "He left for the country with the Borde family almost as soon as I sent my note."

Gabrielle's heart sank. "Oh." So this wouldn't be helping her catch Monsieur Finch's eye. She swallowed but couldn't rid herself of the sinking disappointment.

He squeezed her arm against his side, leaning in. His cologne wafted around her, the comforting notes of cedar and rosemary making her brain hazy. "It will not be a waste of an afternoon. Think of all the conversations you can have with him using your newfound knowledge. The king's architect likes to talk. You will never run out of things to say for the rest of your lives."

The rest of their lives. She imagined sitting in the cramped dining room of Monsieur Finch's tiny London home, solemnly eating dinner while her English husband prattled on about the architecture of London's newest building and all she could interject with was odd facts about Place Louis XV, a subject they'd discussed five hundred times already. It was a bleak picture, and Gabrielle swiftly shook it out of her head. No, that is not how it would go. They'd find many other things to talk about besides just architecture. Surely Finch had other interests.

"Is there something wrong?" Lieutenant Barlow asked.

"*Mais non.*" Her mind was simply muddled by the unexpected savor of his cologne. "We will make the most of the situation."

"That's the spirit."

They arrived near the ambassador, who introduced the king's architect. The man bowed stiffly due to age, but he wore a pleasant smile. Then Lord Stormont introduced his aide, speaking first in French and then in English for the benefit of the young Englishman.

They started off, Gabrielle still on the lieutenant's arm and Madame d'Épinay making her own way amidst the gentlemen. Perhaps Gabrielle should do the same, but the idea of letting go of Lieutenant Barlow didn't sit well. With the unexpected absence of Monsieur Finch, she craved the confidence of holding onto the lieutenant's strong arm.

"Why would he go so suddenly to the country?" Gabrielle whispered as the architect pointed out the long colonnade of the stately Hôtel du Garde-Meuble, which he'd patterned after the colonnade of the Palais du Louvre.

"It is rather like Finch to suddenly change his plans, I am told."

That could play to her disadvantage.

The lieutenant asked something in English over his shoulder. The ambassador's aide said something back with a shrug. Lord Stormont chimed in, earning a laugh from Lieutenant Barlow. She listened intently, but caught very few words. Was that "Finch" they were saying? If so, she'd been saying it entirely wrong and Lieutenant Harvey hadn't corrected her. In fact, he'd mimicked her incorrect pronunciation.

Lieutenant Barlow turned to her and grinned. "Well, that is good news," he said quietly enough the party behind them would not hear.

"What did they say?" Gabrielle asked.

"Were we speaking too quickly for you to understand?"

She dropped her gaze to her fitted hand. "I...don't speak English."

The lieutenant halted, and Gabrielle reddened as they drew confused looks. She tugged on his arm to get him moving again. "Why is that so shocking? We do not all learn it when we are young. I know as an Englishman, that must be hard to believe."

"But you are trying to woo an Englishman and wish to live in his country. I assumed you at least had some knowledge of the language."

"My education was not as complete as it ought to have been." How terrible it sounded. Would he think her beneath Monsieur Finch now? She spoke quickly, attempting to convince him. "There was not as much opportunity for tutors at Amilly. And my parents thought—"

The lieutenant held up a hand. "There are many ways to earn an education, mademoiselle. Is that not correct, Madame d'Épinay?"

"Of course it is!" Madame d'Épinay chimed in without pause. Clearly she had been listening despite their efforts at discretion. Gabrielle wanted to sink into the stones under their feet. If Madame d'Épinay knew her designs, how long would it take for the rest of Paris to know? Could they count on her to keep it secret? If Gabrielle's parents discovered her plan right now, Élisabeth would lock her in the house until she was thirty.

"I did not have a usual education, either," Lieutenant Barlow said. "I was in a ship at war from the time I turned fourteen. We didn't always have time to study our Latin and Greek."

Fourteen. That seemed so young to be participating in men's wars. "But somehow you learned French well."

"That is because I have tried to continue my learning. When I returned from war at eighteen as a new lieutenant without an assignment, I threw myself into my own studies. I took charge of my education."

"I am a woman," Gabrielle said. "I am not..."

Madame d'Épinay's eyebrow shot skyward.

Gabrielle hunched her shoulders. "We are not at liberty in the way men are when it comes to education. Am I wrong?"

The other woman looped her arm through Gabrielle's. "Yes, we have to work harder. But if we do not put in the effort, our daughters and their daughters will be in the same predicament. We must pave the way for the future generations, *mon amie*. It starts with you."

If she could not secure a match, there would be no future generations. Gabrielle's stomach twisted. That was thinking too far ahead. She could not handle the anxiety of education for her posterity at the moment.

"Let us start with English, shall we?" Lieutenant Barlow said. "You must at least learn some helpful words and phrases."

"I thought we were supposed to be learning about architecture this afternoon," Gabrielle muttered.

"Come see me Monday morning, the both of you." Madame d'Épinay let go of Gabrielle's arm. "I would not mind practicing English, if I find myself of the mind to practice Monday. If not, I shall read and you may practice as long as you like." She dropped back behind them to engage Lord Stormont, but not without a cunning smile in their direction.

"A perfect opportunity," the lieutenant said. "How fortunate for us."

Yes, perfect. Now they had a middle-aged matchmaker watching their every move. Did Madame d'Épinay overhear that Gabrielle's object was Monsieur Finch, or did she assume Gabrielle had her sights set on Lieutenant Barlow? The latter was ridiculous. She'd known, or at least known of, Monsieur Finch much longer than Lieutenant Barlow. Monsieur Finch meant to live a cozy, quiet life. Marriage to a military man could only lead to loneliness.

Gabrielle turned her attention to the king's architect, still droning on about the Corinthian columns on the Hôtel de Garde-Meuble. Corinthian columns seemed an important aspect of her architectural education, and they were the perfect way to distract herself from entertaining the thought that perhaps the loneliness was not a bad price to pay if it meant having a husband with so warm a smile and such strong arms as a certain English lieutenant. Paying that idea any mind was preposterous. She had a plan. And nothing, not even Lieutenant Barlow's unconscious effort, would deter her from it.

CHAPTER 8

Harvey paced the courtyard of the embassy. Stormont had called for the carriage to take them to Madame Necker's salon not five minutes ago, and there was still plenty of time before the horses would be brought around. He couldn't sit still, and with Stormont and Finch finishing their preparations, he had no one with whom to pass the time.

His mind drifted back a few days to the afternoon with Mademoiselle d'Amilly at Place Louis XV. It had been a brilliant afternoon, unlike the cloudy and threatening day that had dawned this morning. She had made it all the brighter. How eager she'd been to learn the names of all the features Monsieur Gabriel had mentioned. It was as if their talk with Madame d'Épinay had bolstered her confidence. The mademoiselle wanted to learn. She wanted to know things. Life had held her back for too long.

Harvey's lips ticked upward at the memory of her wide green eyes as she tried to take it all in at once. She felt unworthy—he could see it in her timidity—but every so often a little spark of fire flared out from behind her protective walls, such as when the *philosophes* attempted an attack on the subject of women's reason. He needed to find a way to stoke that fire. If her confidence grew, perhaps she would have the courage to speak with her parents about her plans and solicit their help. After all, Harvey would not be around much longer to help on her quest.

Two more weeks. Harvey kicked at a pebble and watched it scurry across the courtyard. The hum of the crowded rue Jacob, muffled through the gate, made him long for the spacious quiet of the sea. Of course, living quarters in a ship were as cramped as any city, but standing on the deck looking out at the ocean, millions of waves at your feet, it felt as though the world were yours and yours alone. It had been two years since his assignment to a guard ship had ended. What an awful existence by navy standards, but he'd take it over being land bound. Besides the brief passage from Dover to Calais, he'd hardly set foot on a proper ship's deck since.

While he anticipated the chance to board a ship once more and the promise of his own ship to command after he returned, two weeks was hardly enough time for him to truly help Mademoiselle d'Amilly. If Finch had taken the bait Friday last or not flown the coop to spend a few days in the country with his friends, Harvey wouldn't be as worried. After he left, who would Mademoiselle d'Amilly turn to for help? Perhaps Madame d'Épinay? In England, the madame would not be nearly as respected as she was in France, what with all the scandals surrounding her husband and her own liaisons with various *philosophes*, but here she might be the most respected helper Mademoiselle d'Amilly could find. Would Madame d'Épinay get bored of the young Parisian once he'd left? Someone had to help her finish the task of marrying Finch.

As though conjured from his thoughts, Finch appeared at the door. "Is the carriage arriving soon?" he asked.

"I'm not certain," Harvey said, shoving his hands into his breeches pockets. "I thought I had better wait here to make sure it comes at all."

Instead of protesting Harvey's attempt at a joke, Finch nodded thoughtfully as though it were a reasonable possibility. "Do you think Madame Necker will have fish again?" The clerk pulled on his gloves.

Harvey shrugged. "It is still Lent for another week."

"Ah. You are right."

"Mademoiselle d'Amilly looked as disappointed as you with her fish last week." How often could he mention the young lady without drawing suspicion from Finch? Finch's level of obliviousness made it easy to hide his efforts.

"She certainly pushed it around in a similar manner."

So he did notice something about her. That was encouraging. "Mademoiselle d'Amilly seems to be a nice girl," Harvey said. It sounded so inefficient to describe her, but he couldn't sing her praises at this point. Finch was taking it as slowly as a man possibly could.

"She is very pleasant, indeed." Finch clasped his hands behind his back. "Madame Necker was in fine form as always, and I'd forgotten how droll Madame d'Épinay can be."

Harvey closed his eyes when Finch praised the other women but not her. He had a talent for missing points. "Have you seen Mademoiselle d'Amilly often?"

Finch tilted his head toward the cloudy sky. "On occasion. She attends some of the same balls as we do with her mother. Her mother is an interesting woman. A little loud for my comfort. And she always dresses as though she were on her way to a masque at Versailles. So many colors. So many feathers."

Back to the topic of someone else. Heaven help him. "I think she's a lovely young woman to talk to after our walk in Place Louis XV."

"I suppose she is." He perked up. "Was that enlightening? I have met Monsieur Gabriel once before, and his insight was truly fascinating. I would have loved to hear his explanations for the new square."

"Perhaps you should have stayed in Paris and come with us." Never mind Harvey had spent a good deal of time constructing the plan and getting all the players in place—the architect, the ambassador, the female chaperone.

"I cannot say no to the Borde Family. They have been terribly kind to me during my time in Paris."

Harvey tried not to fault him. One should respect one's friends, or they would cease to be friends. But when it meddled with someone's nefarious plans...

Nefarious. Harvey turned toward the embassy's door. He wasn't being nefarious. Securing a match between a hopeless romantic and a lady longing for someone to care about her did not make him a villain. It seemed as though they could make a handsome couple. Both were thoughtful and not vain. They'd fare better than he hoped to with Miss Pratt.

"Is something the matter, Lieutenant?"

Harvey cleared his thoughts with a shake of his head. "Not at all. I simply hope we leave soon. We are bringing Mademoiselle d'Amilly to the Neckers again."

"Very good. Wonder if Madame—"

"She was anxious to speak to you about Monsieur Gabriel's stories," Harvey said quickly.

Finch's brows knit. "I did not know she had an interest in architecture."

No, you dunce. Only an interest in you.

"You know, Madame Borde has taken quite an interest in de Wailly's work."

Harvey pulled his cocked hat off his head. It was all he could do not to throw it. Of all the British ambassador's staff, why had Mademoiselle d'Amilly chosen this one? Finch was an amiable enough man, but he was impossible.

"I must say, your interest in architecture took me by surprise," Finch said.

"Me as well, sir." Harvey returned his hat as a few drops of rain splattered on the cobblestones around them. This evening was not starting well.

Gabrielle startled as someone took her arm and held her back from the group making their way into Madame Necker's salon. She whirled, coming face to face with Lieutenant Barlow. He held a finger to his lips, watching as the footman led the group out of the foyer.

"What is it?" she whispered. He didn't release her arm, which would have made her skin crawl with anyone else. But with him, somehow it made her feel safe.

"Are you sure you wish to continue?" he asked.

"Into the salon? Yes. I think they will be wondering where we are."

He shook his head sharply. "No, I mean pursuing Finch."

Gabrielle could feel the flush rising up her neck, and she prayed no one could hear them. "Do you think I shouldn't?"

He blew out a sharp breath. "I do not think you will succeed."

Gabrielle went cold. Lieutenant Barlow told her he would be her comrade, that he would support her in this quest. Now he was giving up?

"If I told him directly that you had interest in him, I think he would still not understand what I meant," the lieutenant hurried on. "Is he truly the wisest choice of all Stormont's staff?"

She threw up her hands, breaking his grip on her arm. "There is not another on the ambassador's staff I would trust. They are either married or cads, neither of which are good recommendations. You would have me throw myself at one of them instead of a man like Finch? The only good, unmarried man under Stormont's roof?"

She faltered. That wasn't quite right. There were two other good, unmarried men. Stormont himself was an honorable man, though she would never dream of trying to engage herself to him. And then there was Lieutenant Barlow. She swallowed. Was...he suggesting...?

He stared at her as though reading her thoughts, his russet eyes wide. They searched her face, something swirling behind them. Confusion? Regret? She couldn't tell. Her heart beat wildly, and she struggled to draw in a full breath. Could *he* take her away from here? Back with him to England and away from the disaster her stepmother had created here? His gaze flicked to her lips for the briefest of moments. Almost as quickly he straightened, leaning back and blinking rapidly.

Gabrielle put a hand to her stomach. What had just happened? Of course, there was not enough time for Lieutenant Barlow to be the one, nor as favorable a situation as what Finch offered. Something akin to disappointment made her stomach turn. It had to be Finch. She *wanted* it to be Finch.

"I-I hoped to have him practically in your pocket by the time I leave in two weeks," the lieutenant said, brushing at his cream-colored waistcoat. "I don't think that is possible with Finch, and anyone with half a brain can see that."

Had he called her stupid? She pressed her lips together, anger flaring within. "You do not have to help me and my half of a brain," she said. "I was doing well enough before you stepped in."

He lifted his shoulders. "Mademoiselle, I am only trying to—"

"Help. Yes, I know. Though you might do it without insulting my intelligence like the other men." She fixed him with the best smile she could, but she was gritting her teeth more than smiling. Her eyes pricked. She could not cry. Not here in the foyer with this Englishman she hardly knew. His friendly manners and attention had made her forget. She knew Monsieur Finch much better than Lieutenant Barlow, having mingled in the same circles since the clerk arrived in Paris. Soon the lieutenant would be gone. She could not rely on him too much. "Yours is only one opinion, and I still firmly believe that I made the right decision. I am not so much an imbecile that I cannot weigh the facts and choose for myself." Gabrielle curtsied grandly. "I release you from whatever obligations you thought you were under. You've done enough to earn a card party."

He ran a hand through his hair. "Mademoiselle, I did not mean offense. Do you truly think you can do this alone?"

She squared her shoulders, grateful for the extra height she'd managed with her hair that evening that made her as tall as the lieutenant. For once, her height proved an advantage. "No, Lieutenant. I *know* I can."

"Mademoiselle d'Amilly? Lieutenant Barlow?" Madame Necker's voice sounded from down the corridor. "Is everything all right?"

Gabrielle turned on her heel and marched toward their hostess. "Yes. I only had a little mud on my shoe and was trying to clean it off so as not to spoil your fine carpets." As she slipped past, Madame Necker's expression was one of intrigue. Gabrielle wanted to reassure her that nothing untoward had happened in the foyer. Nothing ever would between her and the lieutenant. But just now it was all she could do to keep composed when the only person she thought she could count on to help her had turned out to be a disappointment.

CHAPTER 9

Harvey excused himself to the Neckers' library as soon as dinner was finished. Surely Monsieur Necker had something of interest in his mass of tomes. The longer Harvey searched, the more titles on finance he found. Perhaps lessons in finances would do him well, since he would need to know how best to invest his future wife's dowry until he could capture some prizes. No doubt she would want new furniture and paper for the walls until they could afford something grander than his little Sussex cottage.

He had just settled into a chair with an ominously large volume when the door opened. For the briefest moment, he hoped it would be Mademoiselle d'Amilly coming to reconcile. As much as he hated to admit it, he owed her an apology for his obtuse way of confronting her. He still had plenty of reservations about Finch, but it was unfeeling of him to assume she'd selected Finch without thought. The man would make an excellent husband. If he could remember he was married, which at this point seemed a legitimate worry.

A MATCH GONE AWRY

"There you are, Barlow," the ambassador said. He closed the door and Harvey put his book aside. "I forgot to give you something." The older man fished inside his coat and retrieved a letter. Harvey knew instantly who it was from. Practically the only person he corresponded with these days—Admiral Pratt.

Lord Stormont extended the letter. Harvey tried to hide his aversion as he read the direction. Yes, that was Admiral Pratt's writing.

Harvey broke the seal. How much would he speak of his daughter this time? It was as though he felt he needed to remind Harvey of her merits while he was away. He'd needn't have bothered. Harvey remembered exactly why he was marrying her—to please the admiral, to earn a commission, and to put himself in a position not to get his heart broken. The merits Admiral Pratt had to remind him about held little sway.

Lieutenant Barlow,

I hope this letter finds you well. By now I'm certain you have heard rumors of the act just passed by Parliament against the colonies.

Harvey scowled. He'd heard nothing final yet.

While I fully support their actions, we must all assume that the colonists will not take lightly to the new regulations.

That much was certain.

I wished to know what the general feelings have been about the idea of war across the world. Surely France would not support someone who whole-heartedly embraced the destruction of monarchies as the whisperings from the Americas seem to support.

They are calling the latest legislation against the colonies the Boston Port Act. I think you will easily guess what that entails, and blockading ports means the need for navy ships. Orders are already on their way to Boston and beyond. While we hope, of course, that the colonists will see the error of their ways, I think it naive to expect this to solve our problems.

Blast it. He knew the colonies would not come along quietly despite the great debt England shouldered on their behalf after the last war. Would the admiral call him home already? It would be a relief after the argument in the foyer.

While I have not yet had opportunity to recommend advancement and command, I suggest you be ready to leave at a moment's notice. There may not be much time to get your things in order before a captain is required. I have a marriage license already secured should we need to move quickly in that quarter.

Harvey nearly dropped the letter. A license in place already?

Best of luck, Barlow. I have all hope that we will see you soon and get you settled in a fine ship. Eugenia sends her love, bids you hurry home, etc.

"Not bad news, I hope," the ambassador said, sitting on the edge of one of the library desks.

"It depends if you are a colonist or not." Harvey refolded the letter.

Lord Stormont folded his arms. "Have they done something stupid again?"

Harvey kneaded his brow. "No, Parliament has retaliated. I assume you have heard."

"Ah, yes. We shall see how that plays out for them."

"And for us, since we are the ones who have to deal with the consequences." Harvey planted his elbows on his knees. "Is Parliament trying to start a war? It does not seem that colonists who have the temerity to attack a ship and throw its cargo into the harbor would hide in corners and wallow in self-pity over a complete halt to their way of life."

The ambassador shrugged, though Harvey caught the tense lines around his eyes. "We shall see. This is new territory for Great Britain."

Fire crackled in the hearth, filling the silence for a time. Harvey didn't like the thought of returning to London so soon. He shouldn't care, what with Mademoiselle d'Amilly dismissing his help before dinner. Going back meant the opportunity to advance his career. It also meant matrimony. Not that he would have the chance to enjoy it. If a command came quickly, he'd be off without so much as a wedding trip for Miss Pratt to meet his many brothers and sisters. Miss Pratt wouldn't mind that, though she'd make a show of despondency. She never seemed to truly care whether he was around or wasn't. At least he would be the one going out into the world rather than the forgotten spouse at home. Miss Pratt wouldn't let anyone forget her.

"Mademoiselle d'Amilly seemed a little put out at dinner." The ambassador stood, tucking his hands in his pockets.

"Did she?" Harvey tried to say it as flatly as he could, mimicking Finch's tone when he'd tried to talk about her earlier. In truth, there had been an edge to her speaking and a decided ignoring of him all through the meal despite Harvey sitting directly across from her.

"Lover's quarrel?"

"No!" Harvey sprang to his feet, tucking the letter away. "No. I do not think Mademoiselle d'Amilly is in love with anyone." That wasn't a lie. As much as she liked the thought of Finch, as much as she respected him, she did not love him yet.

"She has certainly been showing interest."

"Yes, well, interest does not always mean anything."

Was interest itself enough? Choosing the best from a list of British clerks was hardly a sound scheme for happiness.

Harvey went to a shelf and exchanged his book for the nearest volume. It wasn't fair of him to question her choice. She was doing the same thing he was, was she not? Attempting to alter her station by tying herself to someone she would not naturally have chosen if given the privilege of time. Neither of them had that privilege. Rather than dissuade her, perhaps he should think of a better way for her to attract Finch's attention. They had to be more creative.

He walked back toward the ambassador, tapping the book against his palm. She didn't want his help. The memory of the indignation in her eyes made his stomach sour.

"Taking up gardening, Barlow?"

Harvey frowned. What did that have to do with anything?

Stormont pointed to the book in his hands. Harvey turned it to the spine. *Les obsérvations d'une jardinage moderne*. Modern gardening. Not an activity many navy men had the ability to take up. "Oh, I took the wrong book, I thought I had taken..."

The ambassador chuckled. "I hope you can find a resolution to whatever is troubling you, my friend. There are more troubling things ahead, it would seem."

Harvey nodded. Much more troubling.

"Now if you'll excuse me, I need to see that Finch is well. He was looking rather green at dinner."

Harvey hadn't noticed. He was too focused on Mademoiselle d'Amilly ignoring him.

"Come down when you can pull yourself away from

modern gardening. I have a feeling there is someone who would like to speak with you." Then he left Harvey in the darkened library trying to decide what the ambassador meant and what he would do to reconcile with his new friend.

GABRIELLE STARED out the window of the Neckers' salon, which overlooked the dark courtyard. Beyond the still gates lay the streets moving with indistinct figures returning home. Nothing moved in the room behind her. All the *philosophes* and other guests had returned home. Madame Necker dozed on her *duchesse* chair while her daughter slept curled up on a sofa near the fire. They were waiting for Gabrielle to leave so they could go to bed.

Tears threatened, burning the skin beneath her eyes. When the ambassador had left to take a terribly ill Monsieur Finch back to the embassy, Gabrielle had assured them Élisabeth would send the carriage, and the Neckers sent a servant to request it right away. The servant returned with a promise the carriage would arrive presently. Now the hands on the mantel clock both pointed near to perfectly upward and the gates still hadn't opened to admit the d'Amilly coach.

She pressed her forehead to the cool glass. How humiliating, to tarry this late when all the other guests had left and not have any power to change it. In London things would be different. She had to believe.

If she even made it to London. Gabrielle bit her lips. Perhaps Lieutenant Barlow was right and she was on a fool's errand. Tonight had gone even worse than the previous salon meeting. Monsieur Finch had stayed in a corner trying not to be ill, and she'd hardly talked to him for fear of making his headache worse. She would see him at the card party in a few days, but how would it be any different than this? Monsieur Finch was not interested in her. She could not force something such as affection.

Stepping quietly, she retrieved her cape and mitts from the foyer and returned to her post at the window. As she tied the cherry cape at her neck, she prayed again that the carriage would arrive soon. The desire to drown the horror of this evening in her warm covers and forget everything in sleep stabbed at her heart. She shouldn't have come. Why had she been so certain she could do this?

Lieutenant Barlow had left with the rest of the ambassador's party. He hadn't even bid *bonsoir*; he'd simply disappeared out the door while everyone was worrying over Monsieur Finch.

Gabrielle pulled her mitts on with sharp tugs. The card party was planned for Thursday evening. One more evening she had to suffer through the ambassador's company. She hoped the lieutenant would be too occupied with meeting her stepmother's acquaintances that she would not see much of him. Wouldn't have to feel his probing looks like she had all of dinner. Monsieur Finch would find someone to talk to about the moulding or the fireplace, no doubt.

The idea of slipping out the door and finding her way home in the dark flashed across her mind, but she'd be a simpleton to do something like that. If Élisabeth hadn't come in and tried to style them as *noblesse*, moving them to Paris and making her father discontent with simple country life, Gabrielle would be at Amilly, where she might chance a midnight walk. Paris was crowded and filthy.

Unfit for a young woman to find her way home by herself at night.

An iron creak made Gabrielle press her face against the window. A coach! She whispered a prayer of relief. At last she could put this night behind her. Her rapid breath puffed against glass as the two horses trotted into the courtyard. Gabrielle rested her fingers on the window's muntins like a child peeking through a *pâtisserie* window. Élisabeth had come to her rescue for once. The driver slowed the steeds as they pulled parallel to the front door. She mulled how easily she could creep out without waking the Neckers and prolonging the awkwardness of her situation. She would send a note of gratitude first thing in the morning.

Light from the lamps flanking the door caught the carriage's livery as it turned. Gold paint glimmered against the black sides. That wasn't her parents' carriage. It belonged to the ambassador. She let her arms fall limp to her sides as her heart sank. That wasn't what she needed to see. Why had the ambassador returned at this hour? Could he be persuaded to take her home, even if it was the wrong direction?

Footsteps sounded in the corridor above and started down the stairs. Gabrielle tiptoed from the room. She would ask Monsieur Necker and the ambassador for help. Perhaps the Neckers' coach had returned from taking Monsieur d'Alembert home and she could beg him to use it before the servants put it away at the back of the house. The man arrived at the bottom of the stairs just as she reached the foyer.

"Monsieur, would..." she began. It was not Monsieur Necker, but a solemn Lieutenant Barlow. Gabrielle clamped her mouth shut. She could have sworn she saw him leave with the rest of the ambassador's party, but here he was.

They must have left to take Finch home quickly and sent the carriage back for Lieutenant Barlow.

"Your carriage still hasn't come." Concern flickered across his otherwise stoic features.

Her shoulders sagged. "I'm certain it will arrive shortly," she said, voice thick with uncertainty. He saw straight through her horrible attempt at cheerfulness.

"I'll escort you home," he said. The footman had gone off to other duties, so the lieutenant collected his hat and cloak himself. Gabrielle stood mute as he readied to leave. When he'd finished, he opened the door and motioned for her to go through it.

"I've left a note of thanks to the Neckers in the library," he said softly. "It seems they're all asleep in their favorite places."

Gabrielle forced her feet to carry her through the doorway, not looking at him as she passed. After this evening of complete loneliness, the lieutenant had stepped forward to help despite how angry she'd been earlier. He closed the door quietly then took her hand and gently led her down the steps. Only the tap of their shoes on stone and the shifting horses broke the silence of the courtyard.

The lieutenant opened the coach and paused, turning to face her. The light of the mostly full moon painted his face with a silvery glow.

"I am sorry for our earlier conversation," he said.

She looked down at his hand still supporting hers, her shoulders hunching. "You need not be. You had every right to express your concerns."

"I did not express them well. I questioned your judgment when I should not have."

He was apologizing, and not in a manipulative or condescending way. When was the last time someone had truly apologized to her? "My judgment is not always the best," she said.

"Your judgment is better than you think." He sighed. "I do worry about Finch being your aim. I do not know if he is ready for a wife, financially or intellectually. However, he is kind and eager to please, and I do not think you could ask for more in a husband. Some women are not so lucky in their partner." His voice faltered.

"I am grateful for the help you have given and I do not wish you to feel obligated to continue helping me," she said. "You do not have long in Paris, and you should enjoy it while you are able."

"I am enjoying it."

Gabrielle laughed. He couldn't be serious. "Playing matchmaker?" Along with escort and English tutor. She had thought all evening about canceling their upcoming meeting at Madame d'Épinay's, but that resolve was faltering the longer they spoke.

He smiled, and it chased the chill from the air around them. "Of course. After all, I was a matchmaker before I was assigned to a ship. With my brothers and sisters, of course."

"You must be quite skilled at it, then," Gabrielle said.

"Clearly my skills have rusted from disuse."

Some of the tension in her shoulders dissipated. She tried to imagine this tall, confident man as a little child getting caught up in matchmaking and throwing his older sisters at whatever man seemed most qualified. What did a young boy consider an eligible match? Perhaps she needed a boy like Lieutenant Barlow at her side. Even Lieutenant Barlow, the man, would suffice.

He held out his hand for hers. "I did not intend to imply you were stupid, though that is practically what I said. I hope you'll forgive me."

She rested her hand in his, and the feeling of rightness and comfort that flowed into her made her forget to respond for a moment. He helped her into the coach and climbed in behind her, then he rapped on the roof. As they started away, she said, "I do forgive you."

She could just make out his smile in the dark. "I am glad of it. And I hope to not have to ask you for forgiveness again."

"I think in most friendships one must ask for forgiveness at some time or other. At least in the friendships that matter."

The seat creaked as he shifted. "And this is a friendship that matters to me."

"It matters to me as well." She turned toward the window, overcome by a strange feeling she couldn't describe. A feeling that whispered his friendship mattered more than she wanted to admit. They needed to change the subject before this expanding sensation in her chest made her say something that would only confuse the both of them. "Why did you not leave with the ambassador earlier?"

"I was worried you wouldn't have a way to get home. Though I've never met her, I've gathered that your stepmother can't often be trusted."

She hugged herself, hating how the truth sounded when spoken aloud. "I had hoped she would follow through this once." A foolish notion.

"We all have to face someone like that in our lives," the lieutenant said. "My father is such a man. He told me time and again he would assist me in finding a house to call my own so that I could marry while peace prevailed. He was to give me a portion of my small inheritance to help fund it as well." He drummed his fingers on the leather seat. "In the end, it fell on me to locate the house and come up with the funds on my own."

Gabrielle's heart broke. He knew as well as she did what it meant to be ignored by someone who should have cared. "This is your cottage in Sussex?"

"Yes. Downham Cottage."

"I hope you are happy with your choice," she said. Oh, to be back in the country. It seemed like a distant heaven.

He leaned forward, resting his elbows on his knees. "In the end, I am pleased with it. The house is all my own, rather than a place my father influenced me to take."

"How free that must feel, to have a space of one's own," she said, leaning forward as well as though guided like a horse on invisible reins. She liked to be close to Lieutenant Barlow. Something about his presence calmed and excited her all at once.

"It is my favorite place on land," he said. "Though it will not be all mine for long."

He meant when he married. Gabrielle pulled back, not enjoying the thought of some unknown English girl running his household. "Tell me about the cottage," she said. "Is there a *pâtisserie* nearby?"

He tilted his head to the side, the moonlight catching his hair. "How could there not be? You know me better than that, mademoiselle. It was one of my highest priorities."

She laughed, hiding her mouth behind her hand. It felt good to laugh after the events of the evening. It felt even better to be on good terms with Lieutenant Barlow once again. As he told of the flower gardens and the country landscapes, a longing panged in her heart for this home she'd never seen. And likely never would.

Most likely it was her tiredness that was making her feel so odd tonight, pining for places that had little connection to her. It had to be partly her regret for her former countryside home as well. She laid her head against the back of the seat as the lieutenant continued on in his soothing voice and she drifted into dreams of lilacs and quaint houses and a handsome lieutenant with a warm grin. Whoever did catch his eye would be the most fortunate girl indeed.

CHAPTER 10

Harvey rose to his feet, relief sending a smile to his face as Mademoiselle d'Amilly walked through the door of Madame d'Épinay's library. They hadn't spoken much in the coach on the way home from Madame Necker's—she'd fallen asleep against the side before they'd arrived at her house—but the fact she'd forgiven him was a good sign. She had seemed at ease before her slumber, and that prevented him from completely losing hope. Still, he'd been second-guessing himself the last two days over whether she would come as agreed upon.

"I am 'ere for my English lesson," she said in timid English.

Harvey swallowed a laugh at her pronunciation. He didn't want her to think he was laughing at her, because he wasn't. In reality, there was something rather adorable about her thick accent, and he couldn't quite contain the strange emotion that filled him when he heard her speak his native tongue.

"You already know a little, then?" He reached for the

basket she carried over one arm and she allowed him to set it on the side table nearby.

"Our footman told me to say that. I hope I said it correctly."

"You are brave to trust the footman. What if he deceived you?"

She paled, clasping her hands in front of her. "Have I said something rude?"

"Your trust was not misplaced. You said you were here for your English lesson."

The mademoiselle relaxed her stance. "There are only so many people I can trust. I cannot afford to misplace it."

Madame d'Épinay trailed in after her. "I'll just be in the corner reading. No English for me today. I haven't the mind for it. But do not let me disturb you." The woman sauntered over to a large velvet chair at the opposite end of the room and plopped into it.

"*Merci,* madame," Harvey said, then motioned to the chair next to his. He'd hoped she would say something similar. "Shall we sit?"

Mademoiselle d'Amilly took the offered chair. She wore a green hooded jacket this morning. A Brunswick, he thought they were called in England. It emphasized the color of her eyes and hugged her curves in a very flattering way. "This isn't your stepmother's." He motioned to the jacket.

"Oh, no. It isn't." She smoothed the jacket's skirt. "Élisabeth prefers that I wear her unwanted things, but I have a few older clothes of mine she hasn't made me dispose of."

"Why is that?"

She shrugged. "I think it makes her feel generous."

Harvey took a piece of paper from a little side table, shaking his head. She couldn't even wear the clothes she wanted to. One more reason of many to get her away from Paris. "Shall we begin?" he asked.

"Yes, please."

"Speaking will be more important in the beginning, I believe, but we will still look at written English a little. I've come up with a list of several vital phrases you will need." He pointed to the first one. "Good morning," he said in English.

Mademoiselle d'Amilly repeated it.

"*Très bien*," he said. "This is the phrase you use in the morning. Literally it means *bon matin*, though you don't use that phrase in French."

"I see." She leaned in to study the phrase. "Good morning. Goooood morning. Good morning. Is that right?"

"Excellent." Why was her voice making him feel this way? A sort of lightness, merriness, and compassion all rolled into one. He wanted to laugh and smile and never stop. He couldn't, though. She would think he was mocking her.

"This one is," he spotted his finger down the list, "'How do you do?'"

"'Ow do... 'Ow do you...' She frowned. "That isn't right. Say it again."

"'How do you do?' It is the same as '*Comment allez-vous?*'"

"'Ow do you do?" She sighed. "It does not sound the same when I say it."

"In England, we like to say the H." He tapped the letter at the beginning of the phrase. "At least some of us do."

"Your given name starts with H," she said. "You wrote it on the note you sent."

"Yes, it does."

She cocked her head. "What is your name?"

"Harvey." He slipped a pencil from his pocket and wrote it for her on the top of the paper. "Hhhhharvey. As though you are blowing on a cold window to fog the glass."

She grinned. "Or blowing on your hands to warm them." She practiced the sound a few times and Harvey joined in. Madame d'Épinay threw them a curious glance, which set them both laughing. Mademoiselle d'Amilly's was that same mirthful laugh she'd awarded Finch when he finally succeeded at saying something funny. Harvey sat back in his chair, hand covering the smile that wouldn't leave.

When her laugh had died out, she took a deep breath. "Harvey." She overemphasized the H, but his name was recognizable on her soft lips.

"Yes?"

"Is that correct?"

He blinked, straightening. "Oh, yes. Very well done." For a moment his mind had escaped him, lost in the sound of her voice and the lovely picture she made sitting beside him. The pale light filtering through the window brought out the flush of her cheeks and the sheen of her hair, like warm chocolate on a cool morning.

"Harvey. Harvey Barlow. Lieutenant Harvey Barlow." She said it aloud to herself, and he didn't dare correct her French pronunciation of lieutenant, which was very different from the English version of the word. She might be learning English, but he did not want her to lose her Frenchness. She continued to murmur his name, correcting herself when she forgot the H sound.

He should have stopped her and had her practice Finch's name, but he shushed his conscience. It had been a long time since he'd heard someone say his Christian name.

"Harvey. I like the name," Mademoiselle d'Amilly said. "Though, I shall have to practice it."

"It is fortunate for you that Gabrielle is similar in English." He retrieved the list. They were supposed to be helping her catch Finch's attention.

"What is the next phrase?" she asked.

"One of utmost importance." Harvey held it out so she could see and pointed to each word as he said it. "'Where is the pastry shop?'"

She gave him a suspicious look. "What does that mean?"

"'*Où se trouve la pâtisserie?*'"

The corners of her mouth curled slyly, and she pulled away the cloth that was covering her basket. "*On la trouve ici!*"

It's here? Harvey peered into the basket. A mound of light cakes, their edges barely brown and tops golden, took up the entire basket. A whiff of orange flower caught his nose.

"Macarons?" His mouth started watering the moment he said it.

"Our cook has been making many sweet things for the card party on Thursday." Mademoiselle d'Amilly nudged the basket toward him. "I know you love pastries. Take one."

Harvey didn't have the heart to tell her Finch didn't love sweets. He plucked one out of the pile and sank his teeth into the tender cake with its crisp outer shell.

"Delicious?" she asked hopefully.

Harvey could only nod with his mouth full. Finch and his silly taste preferences didn't deserve a woman like this. And for a fleeting moment Harvey wished *he* was the one who did.

Harvey sat at breakfast with Finch, Stormont, and a couple others of the ambassador's staff, most of whom had their noses buried in newspapers. Today more than most days he knew the news would not hold his attention. It meant that he mostly stared at the back of a whole forest of newspapers. So this was why the French criticized the practice so much. The newsprint stood as a barricade to intelligent conversation over breakfast.

He glanced down at his plate of cold beef and gammon, complemented by a *petit pain* and a hearty pat of butter. Perhaps he'd picked up the habit of avoiding the papers at breakfast when aboard his last ship, HMS *Seville*, but he found his breakfast much more enjoyable without the journals. This morning, however, he needed to brave the forest and uncover Finch's weakness.

"How soon shall we leave for the card party this evening?" he asked, taking up a bite of beef. Not as salty as it came on ships. This French beef was fine enough, but nothing beat the roast beef of Old England.

"Oh, not earlier than six o'clock, I should think," the ambassador said, not looking up from the London Gazette.

Harvey washed down the beef with a little small beer. "What am I to do until six o'clock?" he wondered aloud. Gabrielle—Mademoiselle d'Amilly, that is—was helping her stepmother with preparations and couldn't pull herself away. He'd already asked.

"There is the École Militaire and the Champs de Mars. You might enjoy that with your military history." Finch took a sip of coffee. "Monsieur Gabriel designed the building."

Perhaps he should be interested in the military training of his former enemies given they might soon become enemies again, but it held little sway today. "Where do you go when you are not tied up with your duties, Finch?"

The young man turned over a page. "There are a few cafés nearby."

Harvey clenched his knife. That wasn't helpful. He cut a bite of gammon. A bit better than the beef. "I was thinking something a little more..."

"Cultural?" Finch volunteered. "I do love the gallery at the Luxembourg Palace. It isn't open today, however. Only Wednesdays and Saturdays, I believe."

Now that was closer to what he was after. "Do you enjoy the arts?" Harvey asked.

"Can a person not enjoy the arts?" Finch lowered his paper. "I remember there being a lovely seascape by le Lorrain. Even you could enjoy that."

Just because he wasn't often exposed to the arts did not mean he did not enjoy them. Harvey broke open the *petit pain* and pulled off a bite as he tried to formulate his next move in the conversation. These rolls were superior to most in Great Britain. He could give the French that. And their butter... He slathered on a generous amount before popping it into his mouth. Somehow it was more savory in Paris.

"Were you thinking of taking someone there?" Finch asked.

Harvey swallowed quickly. "No one in particular." A small gathering would be preferable, if he could find a time some of the staff were not busy.

"Art is sometimes best enjoyed alone."

That wasn't what he meant at all. He didn't come to Paris for the art, fine as it was. And he wouldn't be staying because of it either. "But if friends can be found, surely that makes for better conversation and therefore an increase in enlightenment gained from the art."

Finch looked thoughtfully toward the ceiling. "I think that is very true, Lieutenant. How wise." Then he raised his newspaper again.

Harvey sat back, surveying the mostly quiet table serenaded by the whisper of a turning page and clink of cutlery on china. Wardroom dinners on board were much more lively than this. He hadn't minded the last few weeks, having eaten quickly and before a majority of the embassy's occupants rose. Most days he'd needed to be off meeting the admiral's list of connections throughout the city, but today it thwarted his objective.

He studied the paper Finch was reading. What had Stormont said about Finch? That he got lovesick over dinner invitations? Certainly it was hyperbole, but there had to be truth somewhere in the joke. A card party invitation hadn't done the trick, but perhaps that hadn't occurred because the invitation itself was sent by her stepmother. Harvey's eyes fell on an advertisement for an opera. He squinted, trying to read the small print. *Iphigénie en Aulide* put to music by Monsieur Gluck.

"Have you attended any of Gluck's operas?" he asked.

"Not in Paris." Finch turned his newspaper around to read the advertisement for himself. "I've been to a couple of Monsigny's. Those were quite amusing."

Harvey thought he'd seen the word "*tragédie*" in the advertisement and wasn't certain this one would be quite as amusing, but it seemed a superb place to spark romance. A dark theatre, moving music, emotional story. He had never been to the opera, but from what he had gathered of his sisters and brothers' stories, Finch would be hopelessly lost if they played their cards correctly.

"I have been invited to attend the premiere of *Iphigénie en Aulide*," the ambassador said, finally putting down his paper. "The *dauphine* has secured me a loge to ensure I am there." He laughed. "It is a shame you will have already left, Lieutenant. The *dauphine* herself has had a hand in the creation of this opera. I am quite looking forward to it."

Harvey took another drink, mind racing. If Marie Antoinette helped to write the opera, surely there would be some romance, wouldn't there? He needed to ensure that Gabrielle d'Amilly was in that loge with the ambassador's party. Finch would not invite her on his own unless something incredible happened at the card party. Given their record, he couldn't count on that.

Another thought hit him, and he paused. It also meant there would be many of the *noblesse* mingling. Who better to know France's thoughts on the trouble with the colonies than those who followed around the crown prince's wife? That seemed a fair reason to stay. Admiral Pratt would understand a little delay. Miss Pratt would not mind one way or the other. And he would be able to insist on Gabrielle being a member of their party for the opera.

He lowered his cup and cleared his throat. "I have decided to delay my departure by a few weeks, if that is acceptable sir."

"Delay it?" Finch asked. "Whatever for?"

Harvey shrugged. "The admiral does not have immediate need of me."

"We will enjoy whatever time we have with you, of course," the ambassador said. "It only seemed that with tensions rising in the colonies, he would want you at home."

"The colonies do not even know they are in trouble yet."

At least they didn't have official word of it. It would take several more weeks for the news to cross the Atlantic.

Stormont nodded slowly. "You are enjoying your stay in Paris so much as to warrant an extension." He motioned a footman to refill his coffee cup. "I am very glad to hear it."

Something in his jolly tone made it sound as though he knew something he wasn't sharing. He threw Harvey an amused look, a hint of a question in his twinkling eyes. Unnerved, Harvey turned his attention back to his breakfast.

Finch stood quickly, rattling the table. "I am off to pay a visit to Monsieur Borde." He wiped his mouth on his napkin and laid it on the table. Then he fiddled with the ruffles of his shirt. Satisfied, he nodded to the breakfasters. "If you will excuse me, gentlemen," he said, striding lightly from the dining room.

"He pays visits to Monsieur Borde rather frequently," Harvey remarked, a bite of *petit pain* raised to his mouth. He couldn't make sense of the man's actions and the way he flitted from one topic to the next, from one place to the next, like a butterfly among the May trees.

"It would seem the embassy has become a Forest of Arden," Stormont muttered.

Arden? Before he could ask what the ambassador meant, the man engaged another of his clerks in a conversation about one of the other ambassadors, leaving Harvey to contemplate the task at hand and how he would excuse his absence in England to his admiral and his future wife. Perhaps Gabrielle would have an idea of what he could say.

Gabrielle. Why did his brain insist on using her Christian name? It brought a grin to his face, that was why. And the hours until the card party couldn't pass rapidly enough. Perhaps he should consult her on what to write in the letter to Admiral Pratt. That would give him an excuse to arrive earlier. He'd bring flowers to pardon himself for being so early. A fine plan. He glanced at the clock on the mantel behind the ambassador. Only one thing remained to be decided—what was the difference between early and far too early?

CHAPTER 11

Gabrielle sat by the window, her light blue dressing gown tied over her chemise and stays, furiously completing stitch after stitch. Perhaps the day before the card party hadn't been the best time to decide to remake her gown, but here she was trying to finish before it started in a few hours. The soft pink silk draped across her lap and spilled onto the floor, where her shears lay open and her sewing basket lay on its side.

She listened for the sound of footsteps signaling that the hairdresser had finished with Élisabeth and was ready to start on her hair. Madeleine, the maid who had been forced to play both lady's maid and house maid since their financial state took a turn for the worse, had poked her head in and given Gabrielle an incredulous look twice in the last hour. All things considered, she had worked very quickly, taking in the upper part of the bodice's front panels to cut down the looseness about her chest. Late last night she'd picked out the bodice hem and lengthened it as much as she dared without compromising the seam. Today she had cut a strip of ruffle from the hem of her petticoat and was adding it to the bottom of the bodice for extra length. All that was left was to finish the edge of the ruffle so it didn't fray all over the salon.

Perhaps this stroke of boldness would give her the courage to tackle the rest of Élisabeth's old gowns to make them fit better. Otherwise it would scare her away from ever picking up a needle again. If Élisabeth realized what she'd done, there might be trouble. She couldn't think about that right now. She flipped her braid over her shoulder and pressed on. This work would make her go crosseyed, but if it earned her a little of Monsieur Finch's notice, it would be worth it. All she wanted was a look like the one Lieutenant Barlow had given her when she descended the stairs before leaving for Madame Necker's.

She paused, needle piercing the fabric. No one had ever looked at her like that before. Fluttering filled her stomach like silk petticoats rustling along a dance set. She hoped Finch would gaze at her with the same enchantment, especially if they wed. It wasn't too much to ask, was it? Because in that moment, she had felt like a masterpiece. She knew, deep down, that she was nothing close to stunning. Knowing Élisabeth had taught her that there were so many more important things than beauty. But surely it was not a terrible thing to want to feel lovely once in a while and to know that one person in the world thought you were lovely, too.

Gabrielle pulled the needle through with too much vigor, and it slipped out of her hands and fell to the floor. Not again. She laid aside the gown and got to her knees, feeling for the needle in the lines of the wood floor. She'd forgotten how much she hated this part of sewing—the little pointy slivers of metal that poked you if you weren't careful. If she didn't find it now, she knew she'd find it in the middle of the night with stockinged feet.

A knock cracked against the door, and before she could answer, the hairdresser burst into the room. "*Bonjour, mademoiselle,*" he muttered. Right on his heels was a tall form in a shade of blue she'd come to adore.

"Lieutenant," she squeaked, leaping to her feet and pulling her dressing gown tighter around her. "What are you doing here?"

He grinned like a schoolboy caught in mischief. "I thought all elegant ladies took visitors at their *toilette*. Especially in Paris."

Gabrielle gulped. They did, but she was far from an elegant lady. The *noblesse* did. Élisabeth did. But Gabrielle d'Amilly had never had anyone other than a maid or the occasional hairdresser attend her as she readied for the evening. She hadn't even dressed for the day, being so consumed with her work this morning. The barely picked over breakfast tray on the bed was evidence of that.

"*Mademoiselle, s'il vous plaît,*" the hairdresser said, motioning to the chair in front of her dressing table.

Madeleine arrived at that moment to set up the dressing screen and pull out her cosmetics. How awkward this was. And yet, there was a small part of her that appreciated the thrill of welcoming a gentleman to her *toilette*. She felt like a little girl allowed to attend a grown up dinner.

"'Ow do you do?" she asked the lieutenant in English. *Fichtre*, that wasn't right. "Hhhhhhow do you do?" She gathered up her dress and took a seat at her dressing table, then motioned for the lieutenant to take the chair by the window

"Very well, thank you." He sat in an easy pose, as though unvexed at her state of dress. "And you?"

"Very well, tank you," she repeated. If he wasn't going to act awkwardly, she would try not to make it awkward.

Madeleine covered her with a powdering gown and the hairdresser arranged jars and brushes on the table. Usually no one paid this much attention to Gabrielle and her appearance. They came to help Élisabeth. Her stepmother must have wanted everything to be perfect. Who knew when they would be able to host a party like this again?

"You are very well?" Lieutenant Barlow leaned forward, examining the floor, then reached for something and held it up. Her needle.

She went to snatch it from him, but at that moment the hairdresser took hold of her braid and began to unravel it none too softly. She had to wait while Lieutenant Barlow handed her the wayward needle.

"Is this the dress you are to wear tonight?" he asked. To her relief, he'd returned to French.

Gabrielle blushed. "I am only trying to improve it a little." She went back to rolling and stitching the hem. "Why have you arrived so early?"

"I thought perhaps we could practice your English before tonight."

"This is an odd time to practice English." Fixing a dress and getting her hair arranged. In her dressing gown. She resisted the urge to pull the neckline tighter again.

"In truth, I have come to ask your advice."

"*My* advice?" What could she have to offer him?

Out of the corner of her eye she saw him fold his hands, resting his elbows on his knees. "I have decided to extend my stay by a few weeks."

She whipped around, earning a grunt from the hairdresser, who sharply snapped her head back into position. She'd been trying not to think about the fact that Lieutenant Barlow's departure loomed ever closer. "Why have you decided to stay?"

He opened his mouth as if to speak, then paused. He rubbed his hands together for a moment. "I cannot say."

Because Madeleine and the hairdresser were present, or because he did not know? "Whatever the reason, I am glad of it." She returned to her sewing, a little faster this time. She hadn't realized how much she did not want him to return to England.

After the hairdresser had brushed in copious amounts of pomatum, he secured a cushion to her head and began wrapping the hair up around it.

"What sort of advice have you need of, now that you have decided to stay?" Hurry, hurry. The time was wasting. She couldn't go downstairs to the card party with a half-finished ruffle on her skirts.

"I am not certain how to tell the admiral I have elected to stay." He motioned to the dress. "Have you another needle?"

"In my sewing box." She waved in its general direction because she couldn't move her head that far to see it. Rummaging sounded, then the scrape of the chair legs on the floor, and in a moment he was at her side, lifting the opposite end of the petticoat onto his lap. He threaded the needle, then borrowed her little sewing shears to clip the thread.

"I did not know you could sew," Gabrielle said. "Though I suppose I should not be surprised."

The lieutenant tried to place one of her thimbles over his finger, but it sat insecurely on the very tip. He tried all his fingers until he got it to fit on his little finger. Not the most helpful finger to have it on. He wiggled his finger, and when it didn't fall off, he shrugged. "There are few tailors at sea. You must learn to either live with an untidy appearance and the punishment that it draws, pay someone to do your repairs for you, or learn to sew in order to repair your clothes yourself. The latter is the best option, in my opinion." He watched her make a few stitches, then started on the opposite end, rolling and securing the ruffle edge.

"I do not think I know the best way to address the admiral," she said. There was that cologne again, woody and fresh. How was she supposed to work like this? "Surely your years in the navy give you a better insight than I have."

"I would rather not be blunt about it. There is the problem that his family most likely will read the letter. I wish it to feel sincere and apologetic..."

"When you might not be as sincere and apologetic as the situation warrants?" she guessed.

"Exactly."

"Perhaps you can say your friends have begged you to extend your stay," she said.

"Have my friends begged me?" He raised an eyebrow.

She pursed her lips. "Please stay, Lieutenant. Paris will be so dull without you." Her heart hammered in her chest as the words seemed to escape her mouth of their own accord. Madame Necker had mentioned begging Monsieur Diderot and Monsieur Grimm to write from Russia. It was not much more forward to beg a friend to stay a while longer. Or arriving on the front steps of the lodgings of a man you thought you intended to marry, as she had right before meeting Lieutenant Barlow.

Intended to marry. There was no "thought." Monsieur Finch was the right man for her. Her resolve wavered the tiniest bit. He would be a fine husband, if she could get him to spare her a thought. So of course she wanted the lieutenant here as long as he could be.

"Tell them you have a friend in need of your judgment on an important matter and you felt duty-bound to oblige." She glanced at him.

"Yes! Yes, that is exactly what I shall tell them. A very dear friend." He met her eyes, and for a moment something akin to liquid gold poured into her core. Bright, hot, mesmerizing.

He was a fast worker, and by the time the hairdresser had secured the height of her hair, he'd made considerable distance along the hem. It was time for the buckle curls, and Gabrielle attempted to stay as still as possible so as not to get stabbed in the scalp by an errant hairpin or burned with the iron. The petticoat rustled against her lap as Lieutenant Barlow continued his task. She could feel his fingers getting steadily closer. For some reason, the closer he got, the harder it was to breathe.

"I have need to powder now, mademoiselle," the hairdresser said. "Perhaps you would prefer to move your gown so it does not get dirty."

"Allow me," the lieutenant said, gathering the rose-colored silk into his arms. Gabrielle stuck her needle in the hem and handed him the rest, her arms brushing against the fine wool of his coat. She'd never seen him in anything except the navy's sapphire hues. She couldn't say she minded, as the blue complemented the brown of his eyes. Even though he wore the same attire, today felt different. There was something about his appearance that seemed almost careful when he'd had more of a carefree air before.

"Was that all you needed?" Gabrielle asked him. The hairdresser handed her a cone-shaped powder mask, which she held up to her face. She peeked at the lieutenant through the eye holes, feeling very much like a gangling heron.

"Yes, that was all."

That wasn't a very serious question, at least not enough to warrant arriving at the card party hours in advance. "Have you need of paper and a pen so you may write to your friends?" Even to her ears, her voice was muffled.

Lieutenant Barlow held up the gown. "I have this to help finish first."

"You do not have to finish that." A cloud of powder rose from behind her, and she quickly shut her eyes. The world was all the scent of the mask's old leather and the clunk of the hairdresser's shoes. Powdering always took longer than she liked, but today it was especially burdensome. The powder bellows puffed in her ears. She had the urge to itch the back of her head. Her neck ached from holding still and more than anything she wanted to open her eyes to watch Lieutenant Barlow.

"What do you wish to use to adorn your hair, mademoiselle?"

She hadn't thought much about it in her flurry to finish her gown. "I think the ribbon will be enough."

"We could use some of the flowers," the hairdresser said. "They are a nice color."

"Of course," the lieutenant said. "That would be very lovely."

Flowers? Élisabeth must have ordered them for her hair and had some extras. It meant she would match her stepmother, but there were worse things. "A few would be perfect."

"You there, get the fullest blooms."

Madeleine's footsteps sounded behind them going toward the bedside table as the hairdresser continued to puff and smooth the powder. He laid a curl along each side of her neck. When Madeleine returned, the man fussed with a spot on the top of her coiffure, then he stepped back. "*Voilà*. You may put the mask down now."

Gabrielle lowered the leather cone. In the mirror she stared at rows of curls, with a few braids visible at the back when she turned her head. Three pink roses nestled into her hair, softening the look.

"Is it satisfactory?" the hairdresser asked.

It was more extravagant than anything she'd ever worn, though that wasn't saying very much. She needed her cosmetics to bring her face to a state that matched her hair. "I think..." It would look much better on someone else, but she couldn't say that.

"It's perfect." The lieutenant beamed.

Perfect? No one had ever said that about her before. Why had he come here, saying such nice things and making her feel this way? He must be building her confidence for an evening of trying to impress Monsieur Finch. Yes, that was it. He had no other reason to say these things. She had not heard these sorts of compliments for some time, and that was why this odd lightness kept flaring in her chest nearly every time he spoke. How selfish of her to wish he'd keep talking. She should want to be hearing sweet things from Monsieur Finch and *only* him.

"Come, let us finish this together," Lieutenant Barlow said, bringing the gown back over while the hairdresser fussed over her hair one last time.

Together. She very much liked that word.

IF FINCH DIDN'T SEE this and fall on his face, Harvey had no confidence in the man's judgment. When Gabrielle stepped from behind the dressing screen, he had no words to describe the scene. He could only jump to his feet. The pink gown, with her adjustments, seemed made for her. The ruffles marching along the hems of her bodice and petticoat made the ensemble elegant but not overly extravagant like some fine ladies' clothes. A square neckline and ruffled half sleeves added nicely to the gown. Her hair was lovely, powdered to a soft dove color. Her stiffness when the hairdresser had asked what she thought told him she considered it too much, and while he could agree it did not quite feel like it suited her taste, it looked well on her all the same.

"You will stop a fair number of hearts when you step into the room," he said. She'd almost stopped his.

"Don't be ridiculous, 'Arvey."

Harvey blinked. Had she just used his given name? Or had she said a word he didn't recognize?

Her hand flew to her lips. "Oh! I am sorry. I do not know why I called you that."

"It is because that is the most natural phrase to say with the name Harvey," he said. "At least, that is what I would conclude because seventeen brothers and sisters have said it to me my entire life—'Don't be ridiculous, Harvey.'"

"Seventeen," she murmured. "I still cannot believe that." She turned in a circle, examining her petticoat. "You will forgive me, I hope."

"Only if I may call you Gabrielle." He'd already been doing it in his head.

She tilted her head coyly. "I do not mind."

There. That was what she needed to bottle up for him to douse Finch with—that sunny confidence so fleeting amongst her clouds of timidity. The man wouldn't stand a chance. She was a worthy catch, even if she did not see it. A part of him wished he had a chance at stealing the catch.

What a horrible thing to consider, when he was near to engaging himself to Miss Pratt. A pit formed in his stomach. Was that the real reason he wanted to stay in Paris? To push off the marriage agreement and preparations? Arrangements for war came second nature to him, but those for domestic felicity made him want to run.

Satisfied her ruffle was sufficiently hemmed, Gabrielle turned back to him. "We have things to discuss before going downstairs."

Panic shot through him. She'd noticed his shameless flirtations. Would she put him in his place and remind him of their tasks, or would she rebuke his words as silly and untrue? He'd meant every one of them.

"It's about my stepmothers' family. Monsieur Rouvroy has a temper, so I would advise not to approach him until he has had a drink or two. But do not wait until the end of the evening, because he passes from irritable to drunk to asleep on the *chaise-longue* in little more than an hour some evenings."

Monsieur Rouvroy. Catch him early, but not too early. He added it to the list in his mind.

"The de Vintimilles do not like to associate with guests they have not expressly requested to meet. Watch for them to strike up a conversation with the ambassador. Everyone respects him because he has the *dauphine*'s favor, and Madame de Vintimille insisted he be invited. They will not be rude when he is around. If you can gain their respect during the conversation, all the better."

"Anything else?" This was beginning to seem as though

this would take the entirety of the evening. He needed time to help her with Finch.

"Only one." She took a step closer, eyes wide with sincerity. "Do not associate with Monsieur Goncourt."

"And why is—"

"Mademoiselle!" the servant hissed, head inclined toward the door. "Your mother."

Footsteps clipped down the hall. Gabrielle went pale as a new jib. She grabbed Harvey by his arms and pushed him toward the dressing screen. "She cannot find you in here."

"This is hardly untoward," he said, allowing her to rush him back into the corner of the room. He did not get shoved around by women very much these days.

"As though men haven't been found at her *toilette*," the maid muttered.

Gabrielle released him when she'd put him far enough back he couldn't be seen by anyone entering the door. "I am very sorry. She will not let me hear the end of it if she sees you."

Harvey held up his hands. "Understood."

"Please duck your head," she said, then scurried out from behind the screen.

Harvey glanced at the wooden frame, covered in painted landscapes that were fading. He was a little tall for this, wasn't he? It was fortunate he'd been seated when Gabrielle had changed into her gown a moment ago.

"Ah! But you look ravishing this evening," came a shrill voice. Harvey fought the urge to cover his ears. "Do you see? This dress fits you adequately. You really should stop complaining that my clothes are not suitable. You are simply ungrateful for my sacrifice."

"Thank you, Élisabeth."

Why didn't she correct her stepmother? Gabrielle had worked hard to make the dress suitable.

"There was something I wished to say to you before we go down tonight. What was it?" The footsteps, with their sharp, cracking heels, wandered closer to the dressing screen. Harvey hunched farther down.

"A change in the guest list?" Gabrielle asked.

"No, not that." The woman stopped not far from the screen. A mountain of pearls, flowers, and feathers poking out over the top of the wood marked her nearness. "It was about guests, however. Yes, I remember now. You have been spending a terrible amount of time with those Englishmen lately."

"I…I thought you would approve. The *dauphine* calls Lord Stormont her '*bel anglais*', after all."

Madame d'Amilly snorted. "Yes, well, I think you've had enough diversion with the English. We are at war, remember."

"I told you we haven't been at war for ten years."

"We're always at war with the English, *mon petit canard*." Her little duck? Harvey made a face. "What a fool you are."

Harvey wanted to spring from his hiding place. If he'd had his sword, he might have brandished it. The woman's tone dripped with condescension. So this was what Gabrielle had to put up with day after day.

"I want you to pay attention to Monsieur Longueville."

"The banker?"

"No, his son. Don't be ridiculous. The young Monsieur Longueville is looking for a wife."

"He's despicable," Gabrielle murmured.

"Oh, that hardly matters when it comes to marriage. We just need a fine inheritance."

We. Harvey rubbed his eyes. It was fortunate for Finch they would return to England for good eventually and not see much of his mother-in-law again.

"Come down and help me greet the guests. Monsieur Goncourt is to arrive at any moment." The flamboyant mound of hair disappeared from his sight as footsteps made for the door.

"I will come down in a moment. I haven't put on my necklace."

"Hurry! My, but you are slow. Madeleine, help her." The door slammed shut, rattling the windows.

Harvey poked his head out from behind the screen. Gabrielle flushed, rubbing one of her arms. "I apologize that you had to hear that."

"I'm certain I will hear worse things this evening." What an insufferable woman. "Monsieur Goncourt. The one with whom I am not to associate."

"My stepmother's latest..." She sighed deeply. "Fascination, if you will."

No wonder she'd throw herself into a marriage with a man she hardly knew. Perhaps if they made no headway tonight with Finch, he could... Wait. What was he thinking? He couldn't marry Gabrielle when he was practically engaged to Miss Pratt. Harvey shoved his hands in his pockets, hoping his thoughts were not displayed on his face. Miss Pratt was his ticket to an advancement after all these years. Their marriage would land him a ship, whether England went to war with the colonies or not. He couldn't turn that away because he felt sorry for a French woman in a horrid situation.

His fingers hit something cool, and he pulled the little coin from his pocket. A farthing. He turned it over, tracing the figure of Brittania on the coin's surface. Without thinking, he tossed the coin to Gabrielle.

She yelped in surprise but caught it. "What is this?"

"We call it a farthing. It's for good luck. We put them under the mainmast on ships when they are built. I thought you could use a little luck tonight."

The hint of a smile flickered across her face, then grew as she studied the coin. "I suppose I could."

"You will do wonderfully. Just remember that you are more than how that woman treats you."

"You do not have to be this kind, 'Arvey." She shook her head, curls bouncing. "Hhhhharvey."

Harvey laughed. "It comes easily around you."

Gabrielle turned away, clutching the coin to her heart. The maid watched them curiously from the dressing table, where she'd laid out Gabrielle's jewelry. After a moment, Gabrielle looked at him again, holding up the farthing.

"What is it?" he asked. Surely she wouldn't give it back already.

"I have found myself in the awkward situation of not having a mast." She kept her face stern and serious, but her eyes sparkled with mirth.

Harvey laughed. "Perhaps you will have to put it in your shoe."

She slipped her foot out and dropped the coin into her shoe. "If you do not bring me luck, little coin, I shall throw you into the Seine." She put her shoe back on.

"Not to worry, little farthing," Harvey pretended to call down to the coin. "I expect that Mademoiselle d'Amilly will have every success tonight."

CHAPTER 12

Harvey waited in the vestibule of the d'Amilly family home for the ambassador's party to arrive. Several guests had already made their way into the salon, keeping Madame d'Amilly too occupied to notice he'd arrived before the rest of his companions.

He watched out the window, sliding into the corner when guests arrived so he'd be blocked from view by the door. He didn't want to be seen until it was time. Monsieur Goncourt had sauntered in, as much of a peacock as Harvey had imagined. Avoid him. The Vintimilles also came in a flurry of finery. Take care with them. Gabrielle had told him that despite their connections to the king's illegitimate son, the Vintimilles could be far from genteel. Now he only needed to find Monsieur Rouvroy—the grumpy drunk related to the king's minister—and Monsieur Longueville—the wealthy but despicable suitor. The latter so he could make sure the man stayed far, far away from Gabrielle.

"Harvey," a voice said softly. "They still have not arrived?" As though drawn from his thoughts, Gabrielle appeared with a mist of orange flower scent that tickled his nose.

At that moment, another coach with English livery pulled up to the front steps. "Here they are." At last. Gabrielle scooted closer so she could see out the window, her silk petticoat brushing against him. The first man out of the carriage was Finch, and Gabrielle shifted nervously. Harvey took her elbow and squeezed it to reassure her. She had nothing to fear.

Finch walked stiffly, an ashen look on his face. For a moment Harvey thought he would be sick again and waste another evening. But Finch had had that same expression when he'd returned from the Borde family earlier. He'd been unable to focus on his work when Harvey left. Clearly the man needed some cheering up, and Gabrielle was just the woman to do it.

"I have a very, very good feeling about this evening," Harvey whispered.

Gabrielle raised a brow. Had she caught on to Finch's ill looks? "I hope you know what you are talking about."

When Finch shuffled through the door, he paused, nearly getting knocked over when the footman went to shut it. His eyes clamped on Gabrielle. "Mademoiselle d'Amilly. What a pleasure to see you this evening." His voice held an air of wonder Harvey had been expecting since Gabrielle first showed interest in him. Good. Finch finally bowed after a moment of staring.

She smiled demurely and curtsied. "Hhhow do you do?" she said in English. Her rouge gave her a sweet glow that played prettily with the color of her gown. She was stunning. Harvey's heart swelled with pride.

"Very well, thank you," Finch offered her his arm, which she took. "Have you been learning English?"

Gabrielle glanced at Harvey, and he gave her a slight nod.

"Yes," she said.

"How wonderful!" Finch exclaimed. "Are you—"

"I believe Mademoiselle d'Amilly has only just begun her English lessons, is that correct?" Harvey said, returning the conversation to French. Gabrielle threw him a relieved look. "Perhaps she would enjoy some help with her studies, Finch."

Gabrielle's brows pulled together for the briefest moments before her face returned to a neutral state. She wanted another opportunity to see him, did she not?

"That would be very amusing indeed," Finch said. "I would love to be of assistance."

Harvey trailed them into the salon as Gabrielle and Finch made plans to meet the next week to practice English. What could have opened Finch's eyes so suddenly? For weeks he had been oblivious to the world. Now he was responding to her subtle flirtations exactly the way they wanted from the beginning. He'd be half in love with her by the end of the card party.

As he watched them stroll into the room to greet her mother, Harvey pushed down a niggling feeling in the depths of his heart that he did not like what he was seeing.

Gabrielle sat at a little table across from Monsieur Finch and dealt cards to all four of the occupants. Her grumpy uncle—if he could be called her uncle—sat to her left so that he was teamed with Harvey on her right. She'd warned the enthusiastic lieutenant that it wasn't a good idea to include him as the fourth player, but Harvey insisted. Whatever he wanted to gain through talking to Rouvroy he thought he would get through a game.

"You say this is similar to Whist?" Monsieur Finch asked, a pleasant smile on his face as he watched her deal.

"Yes," Harvey said, "only in *triomphe* you have five cards in a round, not thirteen."

Rouvroy swirled his drink. "You know I despise games of cards, Gabrielle. What I wouldn't give to be at the café just now."

He only despised them for the first hour of a party. By the second hour he was usually loose lipped and willing to play anything. Gabrielle glanced at the old clock in one corner of the room. Guests had arrived three-quarters of an hour ago. It would not be long before her uncle settled into his amiable mood. That must have been Harvey's goal, to get him engaged beforehand in order to have Rouvroy's full attention when he was in a humor to talk.

"This seems as though it will be harder than Whist, despite each round going faster," Monsieur Finch mused. "It is more difficult to keep track of which cards are left over if you do not know which are in play." He winced. "I should warn you, mademoiselle, I am terrible at cards."

"You should not worry, monsieur," she said. She would win it for them.

"Mademoiselle d'Amilly is a gracious hostess," Harvey said, picking up his cards. "She will not mind losing."

Rouvroy harrumphed. "Gabrielle is the best card player in this room. We haven't a chance."

Gabrielle kept her gaze glued to her cards to keep from blushing. She preferred to win quietly. Many thanks, Rouvroy. He hadn't said it to boost her confidence but to complain. She flipped over the top card from the deck to set the trump suit. The queen of hearts. Rouvroy grumbled. Something about it being the wrong suit. Gabrielle rubbed her toe against the farthing in her shoe. Good luck indeed.

"I am the first to start, it would appear," Harvey said, sliding a ten of hearts onto the table.

"Oh, are we supposed to look at our cards now?" Finch asked, straightening in his chair and fumbling with the hand in front of him.

Harvey leaned in to whisper in her ear. "Shall we make a little wager?"

"What sort of wager?"

"The loser has to buy the winner the best treat in all of Paris."

"You are so confident that you will win."

He folded his arms, keeping his cards tight against his cream waistcoat. A competitive fire glowed in his eyes, though it seemed he was attempting to hide it with his relaxed posture.

He didn't know she had the king and ace of hearts.

"I accept your wager, lieutenant. May the luckiest player win." She kept her tone meek, a skill she'd practiced far too often with Élisabeth. Once in a while, she had the chance to use it to her advantage.

She sighed when they arrived at her turn. Of course Harvey would force them all to reveal their trump cards in the first trick. She flicked her ace into the center and won the trick, then started play again with a three of spades. *Please do your part, Monsieur Finch.*

He didn't. He played the two of spades, but after Harvey won the trick for his team, Monsieur Finch revealed he'd had a nine of spades on the next round of play. Gabrielle closed her eyes, resisting the urge to groan.

"Why did you not play that card on the last trick?"

Harvey asked. She could see the laughter he was barely keeping at bay.

Monsieur Finch gave him a blank expression. "I thought I was not supposed to overshadow my lovely partner."

Lovely. That was a step in the right direction. Gabrielle nodded her acknowledgment of the compliment. She would have to forgive him for making winning the game a little more difficult.

"If her card cannot win, then by all means overshadow her," Harvey said. Then he leaned in her direction and mumbled, "If you win because I taught your teammate how to play..."

They would not win because of Finch, but she wasn't about to tell him that. Let him think he had the game in his control.

Clubs was played, and Monsieur Finch made a heartbroken excuse to her for having to play a diamond. That meant he had no clubs nor hearts left. Harvey's brows shot up. He thought he smelled blood, didn't he? Like a hound who imagined he'd caught the scent of a dying fox. What he did not know was the fox had already been turned into a muff. She took the trick with her queen of clubs, then threw down her king of hearts, keeping her face void of emotion.

"I told you she ruled the card tables," Rouvroy grumbled.

Harvey gave a lopsided frown. "That was quite lucky."

"*Eh bien*," she agreed. Harvey dealt the cards, giving her a hand of rather low diamonds, and she nearly despaired until he revealed the trump suit to be diamonds. She easily won all five tricks due to a lack of diamonds in the other players' hands.

"We are two points to none?" Monsieur Finch asked, delighted.

"Three points to none," Harvey grumbled, "because you swept the round."

Gabrielle pulled her fan from her pocket, not because she was terribly warm but because she needed something to distract her so she didn't give him a gloating smile. "We make quite the team, monsieur."

Her uncle, who had been steadily working at his drink during the first two rounds, downed the last of his glass and motioned for a footman to bring another. "We should have played Englishmen against French."

"I believe Great Britain currently holds the winning score," Harvey said, passing all the cards to Monsieur Finch.

"It depends on how far back one traces the history," Rouvroy countered. There was not an edge to his voice. Yet. Gabrielle wasn't sure Harvey had waited long enough.

"The last hundred years, then."

Rouvroy accepted a new glass from the footman and fixed Harvey with a glare. "We shall see how the century finishes."

"Surely..." Gabrielle began, then trailed off. Did she want to join this argument? Not with Rouvroy standing ready to put her in her place. All her stepmother's family did that. He watched her, ready.

"Go on, mademoiselle." Harvey gave her an encouraging wink.

She deserved to be a part of this conversation as much as anyone. She squared her shoulders. "Surely we can hope that the century finishes in peace for both of our countries. That enlightened minds will carry the day, and we will not be forced to bear the burden of war again for quite some time."

"Hear, hear," Monsieur Finch said, dealing the cards methodically.

"A nice thought, *naturellement*," Rouvroy said into his glass. "But the real world does not take kindly to nice ideas."

"If the real world means men in positions of power, perhaps they ought to take the time to listen to the lesser mortals who have to live with the consequences." Gabrielle snapped her fan shut.

Rouvroy sneered. "Careful. You will offend our guests. That is what Britain's colonists are asking."

She hadn't thought of that. The last thing she wanted to accomplish this evening was to offend either Monsieur Finch or Harvey. The clerk appeared unperturbed and the lieutenant was not looking at her. He rubbed his chin, and she wished she knew what was going on behind his russet eyes.

He pulled his cards closer to him but did not pick them up. "Is it not a government's right to tax its citizens to pay its debts, especially for a costly war that benefited the citizens by protecting land and trade?"

"Only some of the citizens are being taxed," Rouvroy pointed out.

"Only some of the citizens were being protected," Harvey countered.

Monsieur Finch gave an uneasy laugh, waving a card in front of them. "It would appear the trump is clubs."

How fitting. Gabrielle arranged her cards in her hand. Very low cards this round. She had to hope Monsieur Finch had a better hand.

Rouvroy picked up his cards one by one. "I like to think France is fair in her dealings with other countries."

Gabrielle winced. His tone implied that Great Britain was not. Rouvroy was not drunk enough yet to be amicable.

"Surely France would not join the colonies if war were

to break out," Harvey said. "Not after enjoying peace for so long."

"You took our land in the Americas." Her uncle flicked a card at the center of the table. "Why should France assist Great Britain?"

Gabrielle couldn't beat the card, so she laid down her lowest, then widened her eyes in a look she hoped spelled "help" to Monsieur Finch. Though she meant it about the game, the discussion was growing louder. Heaven forbid her stepmother come over from her game of Lansquenet and drag Gabrielle back to Monsieur Longueville. Monsieur Finch nodded reassuringly. She prayed that meant he had a fair hand.

Harvey tossed a card in with as much thought as Rouvroy. "I only meant that it would be in France's best interest to remain neutral."

It certainly would be. Dared she hope that France would stay out of it? A war, especially if it happened soon, would complicate her attempts at securing a match. Ambassadors were recalled the moment war broke out, if not before. And Harvey. He would be recalled long before. Her breath caught, and she had to force herself to breathe steadily against the cold that swirled in her chest. Harvey was leaving whether war broke out or not. But no. War would not happen overnight, not with the colonies being so far away. Nothing would prevent him from staying the full length of his visit. The extended length.

Monsieur Finch laughed. "It looks as though I have won the trick." His first time in the game.

"Well done, monsieur," Gabrielle said.

"France has different ideas of what her best interest is than England does," Rouvroy said, drowning out Gabrielle's congratulations.

"Now play a good card," she said in a pause between the heated discussion. Was Harvey sent here to argue? She hadn't considered it a possibility when she'd attempted to set up this meeting. Harvey's calculated prodding seemed so distant from the man who had been just short of adoring her at her *toilette* earlier.

Monsieur Finch nodded, focusing intently on his hand. It was endearing the way he stared, like a puppy deciding the best way to pick up a stick. His face lit up when he decided on a card and laid it down.

Pat, pat, pat. Three more cards fell, and Monsieur Finch gathered up another won trick.

"Ambassador de Vergennes succeeded in causing an uprising in Sweden that put the monarchy back in power two years ago," Rouvroy said, a little quieter but dripping with venom. "He is not afraid to start a war if it would benefit France. And he is not the only ambassador or advisor to the king who would do the same."

A chill ran down Gabrielle's spine. She couldn't be sure if it was the warning in his voice or the thought of men manipulating events in order to start a war.

"It would seem I am having all the luck this round," Monsieur Finch said, stacking their next trick to the side. "The rest of you must have had terrible hands."

"So it would seem," Harvey said, tapping one of his remaining cards against his face. "I did not think Louis XV wanted to enter another war."

"Perhaps he doesn't," Rouvroy said. How did they continue playing while speaking of such things? Gabrielle's head was buzzing, and she'd hardly participated. Her uncle leaned in. "But men cannot live forever, and the men favored by the *dauphin* are not afraid of war."

Harvey's chin dipped in the slightest nod, as though

he'd found something he was looking for. He tossed his card in the pile for Monsieur Finch to collect again. "France thinks she can win?" he asked.

Rouvroy held his gaze so intensely that Gabrielle had to look away. She did not like the ice in his eyes. "Sometimes revenge is more important than victory."

"Come now!" Gabrielle cried, attempting a light voice despite the doom settling in her stomach. "We are here to associate as friends, not enemies. Let us keep the talk of war to other salons."

"Of course," Harvey said as they all laid down their last card. Another victory for Monsieur Finch.

"We won again," the clerk said happily. "That gives us five points, *mademoiselle*. Have we won the whole game?"

Gabrielle forced a smile. "Yes. I knew we would make an excellent team."

"I told you she always wins," grumbled Rouvroy.

She wouldn't have won so easily if they hadn't been distracted by the talk of war. She shivered, even though the room had grown rather warm. France and England at war. They hadn't been at war since she was too young to appreciate the magnitude of such things. Maturity made it much more heavy a matter. Add to that the weight of knowing someone you admired would be sent into harm's way, to possibly be killed at the hands of her own countrymen...

She trailed her eyes along the gold buttons that adorned Harvey's coat, marching down his chest on white lapels. It would be difficult to marry a man of the navy, wouldn't it? To be bound to the land while your heart was set adrift. Even if that land was a pretty little cottage in Sussex with lilacs at the windows and a creaky old door, as he'd said coming home from the Neckers'.

"*Messieurs*," came a crooning voice that snapped

Gabrielle out of her contemplation, "we can hear your arguments from across the room. We do not talk about such serious things here." Élisabeth descended on their little card table, waving her feather fan like the beating of butterfly wings.

"You do not talk about serious things at all." Rouvroy drank deeply from his glass.

Élisabeth cackled. "*Mon frère,* you are so droll. Get another drink and come play Lansquenet, *imbécile.*" She grabbed Gabrielle's arm as all the players rose from their chairs and yanked her close. "I told you not to spend all of your time with the *anglais*," she said in her ear.

"Do not worry." Gabrielle had had enough of the English for the moment. "I will find Monsieur Longueville."

"See that you do." Élisabeth released her and rounded on Harvey. "Lieutenant Barlow, I have not had the honor of playing your partner yet this evening." She sidled up next to him, as much as her voluminous petticoats would allow. "You will not deprive me of this honor, will you?" She tilted her head, eyelashes fluttering.

Gabrielle's stomach soured in an instant. Her heart recoiled. Élisabeth had Harvey in her clutches. She wanted to rip the woman's hand off of his arm and shove her back toward the pack of vipers and leeches that Élisabeth called friends.

Harvey gave her a small wave, his hand at his side so her stepmother couldn't see. He might have intended it to mean he would be fine. Perhaps he wanted to go so that he could argue some more with other Frenchmen who knew people in high places.

As they left, something tapped softly against her arm. "Thank you for being my partner, mademoiselle," Monsieur Finch said. "I greatly enjoyed it."

"I did as well. What an amusing game." She had all his attention, just like she wanted. As though dawn had broken and the man could finally see her after whatever darkness he'd been under the last few weeks.

"I believe I spy a little bowl of *confiserie* among the refreshments," the clerk said, timidly taking her arm. "Shall we borrow it and find a corner to practice your English while we munch on sweetmeats?"

Harvey stood beside Élisabeth's chair talking to Madame and Monsieur de Vintimille, the cousins who were related to the king's illegitimate son. He looked at ease, as he always did, but unlike usual he seemed completely unaware of her. Her stomach twisted even tighter. She shouldn't mind. She had Monsieur Finch. But she couldn't shake the fact that she *did* mind.

Harvey had become so intense during his conversation about war with Rouvroy. Too intense. The way he'd watched her uncle and the way he watched her other relations now, she could see calculations happening in his mind. Even as he pretended to enjoy his time in their midst, he was gleaning information from them. He was a navy officer supposedly without an assignment in Paris who had to report to his admiral about delaying his return from a friendly visit. That seemed highly suspect. What if he was here to investigate for his admiral, and helping her had only been a tool to get to some of the people he needed?

"Yes, I would like very much to practice my English," she said to Monsieur Finch. Something to try to distract her racing mind. Everything Harvey had done, from coming to Paris to agreeing to help her, had been related to war. While most likely he was not at liberty to confirm such things, the thought that his intentions had been wrapped up in something so abhorrent and that he hadn't divulged this fact to her from the start made her ill. What else was he not sharing with her?

Gabrielle allowed Monsieur Finch to lead her away from the crowd. They stopped briefly to retrieve the sweets. Her feet moved woodenly as she followed him to a sofa, her mind nowhere near a place to be able to practice a language as difficult as English.

Why, when Monsieur Finch was finally starting to see the light of something more between them, did she feel like darkness was creeping in?

HARVEY RUBBED AT HIS FOREHEAD, trying to ease the headache he'd developed after having to listen to Madame d'Amilly most of the evening. When she stood to see Monsieur Rouvroy to the door, he sneaked out into the foyer through another door and down a narrow, darkened corridor.

Before his eyes could adjust to the dimness, he ran into a puff of silk. He threw his arm against the wall to steady himself, catching hold of the off-balanced figure before she fell.

"Gabrielle?" What was she doing here?

"*Désolée*, I did not see you." She pushed away from him.

"Are you well?" One didn't hide in dark corners if they were well.

She put distance between them, wrapping her arms around herself. "Yes, of course. I am quite well. I only needed a moment to refresh myself." She spoke tightly as though trying to keep back...something. Tears? Harvey clenched his teeth. Had Finch said something that hurt her? If he had, Harvey would ensure he regretted it.

"I can understand the desire for a little reprieve. Your stepmother is a rare breed. If she fails at securing the social status she desires, she could find work as a bosun's call." His ears were still ringing.

"A what?"

Had he used the right word in French? He tried again. "*Un sifflet*. Used for communication on a ship."

"Oh, yes. I understand." She'd angled herself a little away from him. Even in the darkness, so filled with shadows, gray light shimmered across the surface of her gown. He remembered how she'd commanded the card table at the start of their game. Flirting with Finch. Standing up to Rouvroy. She'd found herself. She didn't need him anymore.

"Did something happen with Finch?"

She shook her head, curls brushing across the curve of her neck. "No. He was perfectly attentive all evening." She sounded too polished. Emotionless.

"I'm glad of it." When Harvey had begun his interrogation of her step-uncle, he had seen her squirm, her eyes sending him silent pleas to stop. Had he caused this? "Was it something I did?"

"Of course not." She licked her lips, giving them a faint shine.

He lowered his voice. "Tell me. Please."

She dipped her chin, studying her hands. "It is nothing. If our countries are to be at war soon, let us enjoy the last happy moments we have as friends."

Yes, it was his conversation. Blast. He should have known. He might have cornered Rouvroy after the game instead of using it as the setting for his conversation. While he hadn't expected the man to engage as intensely as he did, Gabrielle *had* warned him.

"I apologize. I shouldn't have broached the subject at the card table."

"Is that what you are here for?" she said, voice somehow soft and intense at the same time. "To start a war?"

Harvey fiddled with the buttons on his sleeve. He shouldn't admit to it, but it wasn't as though he were on a secret mission for the government. Most of the ambassador's staff had guessed what he was after. "I am here to determine what sort of fight is on the horizon and what we should prepare for."

"You are parading about as a friend. A wolf in sheep's clothing."

He flinched. "That is hardly fair, Gabrielle. I am trying to protect my country in finding out if we can expect France to join the fight." That and put himself in position to earn Admiral Pratt a healthy sum of prize money. He wanted to shrink into the shadows. He should have told her from the beginning why he needed to speak with her relations.

"Your duty to the British crown is commendable," she spat. "I only hope that you can give the same devotion to the woman you love. Whenever it is you find her."

"I don't plan to find a woman to love," he muttered. "Love is a risk I am not up to taking." Hence why he was negotiating for Miss Pratt's hand. A ship for a marriage. How heartless it sounded.

She scowled. "Why do you speak to me of love when you do not care for it yourself?"

Harvey rubbed the back of his neck, his collar suddenly tight. "I may not want to make risks for love, but you deserve to have it."

She gave a mirthless laugh. "That makes little sense." She pulled herself up to her full height. "I suppose this is *adieu*. You spoke to the people you desired to meet. Now you can see what sort of war is in the future."

Why did this feel like the last time he'd see her? "I am still in Paris for a few more weeks."

"But we have no further need to meet."

He folded his arms. "You are angry because of my intentions in regards to meeting your stepmother's family."

"I am frustrated that the only reason you agreed to help me is because of who I knew." She hugged herself again, taking a step back.

He shook his head. "Why does it matter my reasoning? We each had our motives and we made a deal."

She lifted her chin. "And now we have both fulfilled our respective parts of the deal. I bid you *bonsoir*, monsieur."

She couldn't leave like this. He caught her hand. Her skin was smooth as rose petals against his despite how tense her hand was. "Gabrielle."

She whipped her head around to glare at him, but as he whispered her name her face softened.

"I didn't do it just for me," he said. "I wanted you to be happy. I *want* you to be happy."

She nodded slowly. "*Merci, mon ami*." Then she slipped her hand from his and vanished into the foyer.

GABRIELLE SHUFFLED into her room and closed the door. That took more effort than it should have. The fire in her room had died down to barely glimmering coals that faintly outlined the surfaces of her room. Her dressing table, with the sewing basket perched on top. The posts of her bed, whose clarion call made her want to fall into it immediately. The chair by the window where Harvey had sat.

She shook her head, her heavy coiffure unbalancing in her current exhaustion. Madeleine was helping Élisabeth ready for bed and wouldn't be free for quite some time. Gabrielle didn't think she could wait that long. She started pulling pins from her bodice and placing them on the dressing table. Her fingers worked clumsily, but soon she had the bodice off. Then the outer petticoat and inner petticoat and paniers. Then the stays.

For a moment she stood there in a puddle of fabric considering if she could leave it all there until morning. Her body had been drained of energy, but was that because of physical endeavor or a reflection of the state of her mind? She sighed and stepped out of the circle of clothing, then draped the silk gown over the chair. She'd worked too hard on it to leave it on the floor in a crumpled heap. Harvey had worked too hard on it as well.

She lifted the hem and ran her fingers over the stitches he'd made along the ruffle. Not many men would have done that for a lady they loved, much less a simple friend. She'd been unfair to him. He only wished to know France's feelings about the British colonies. That was hardly spy work. He hadn't cheated. He hadn't lied. She let the hem fall back to the chair.

Gabrielle slipped on her dressing gown before taking off her shoes, then bending down to fetch the farthing from the toe. It had been lucky enough. She'd achieved what she'd wanted to achieve. Monsieur Finch had given her a chance that evening. What could have been more romantic of a card party than winning together at *triomphe* and then eating sweets while practicing English phrases such as "Let us walk in the park," and "Would you like some tea?"

Monsieur Finch was a charming man. He knew how to make a lady feel appreciated.

Was it enough? She smoothed her thumb over the image of the monarch and then the image of a Grecian lady on the back of the coin. Slowly she walked to place it on the table near her bed. A vase filled with dark pink or red roses sat atop it. The hairdresser must have left it.

She reached out to pull a rose from her hair to compare them and paused. Élisabeth hadn't had roses in her hair. Surely the hairdresser wouldn't have brought all these flowers just for her. She finished pulling them from her hair and held them up to the vase. Yes, they were the same. A small calling card poked out from under the vase. Gabrielle set the flowers and farthing down and pulled the card out, angling it toward the dim light from the fireplace. "Harvey Barlow," it read in neat print. On the back was a note. She bit her lips, the phantom of that light feeling she'd had earlier manifesting itself in her heart.

Creeping on stockinged feet, Gabrielle made her way to the fire and knelt. She pulled the skirt of her dressing gown to cover her legs. A few timid embers glowed amidst the blackened logs of the previous fire. She plucked a little unburned kindling that had fallen among the ash. The embers only needed a little encouragement. She blew gently, gingerly poking the kindling toward the throbbing lights. Some of the embers caught hold of the kindling, and tiny flames crept along the length. Just enough light.

Settling back on her heels, Gabrielle turned the note toward the light.

This is your moment, mon amie. *I cannot wait to see you shine.*

Affectueusement,
'Arvey

A throb of something—she did not know what to call it—reverberated within her even as she made a face at his tease. She could almost glimpse his face as he wrote it, that carefully guarded grin he hoped she wouldn't see. A person couldn't ask for a better friend.

She set the card on the floor, reading it again as she reached up to pull pins out of her hair. The little mound of pins grew as she worked, and so did her puzzlement. She should be squealing over finally catching Monsieur Finch's eye. When he left, he'd even kissed her hand and asked if she'd attend the Palais du Luxembourg gallery with him next week. She'd gone from barely getting a word from him to focused conversations.

Yet the look Harvey had given her in the corridor stayed at the forefront of her mind. Why had the tenderness of his voice saying her name made her insides tremble so much they hurt? The only people who called her Gabrielle were her parents, and she hadn't heard love in either of their voices when speaking her name for so long. Even her father, who had once been her dearest friend. Had she ever heard it from Élisabeth?

Gabrielle flinched as she scratched her scalp with one of the pins. She glared at the offending metal. Harvey did not have *love* for her. It was friendly affection. The same sort the *philosophes* had for Madame Necker or Madame d'Épinay. He'd told her that romantic love was not for him. A little piece of her heart wanted to prove him wrong.

She brought her legs forward and crossed them, settling in to finish the job of letting down her hair. Her mind was spinning toward thoughts she couldn't entertain. She wouldn't dare find a husband who would leave her alone in a little unfamiliar town while he went off to war in the distant colonies. Never mind that Harvey had chocolate

A MATCH GONE AWRY

eyes and a warm grin, or that he seemed to see her for who she was deep down rather than who she tried to be in front of people, or that he both wanted to protect her and wanted her to stand up for herself. She couldn't deny that.

Her hair started to fall, and eventually she extracted the cushion. With a moan, she massaged her scalp, which had taken up its protest at the maltreatment. She flipped her hair to one side and massaged her stiff neck. Though she couldn't decide what all these muddled feelings meant, she did know one thing for certain. Their deal may have been fulfilled on both sides, but she did not want her acquaintance with Harvey to end. She had so few allies in her world. He was an ally she wanted to keep at her side as long as she possibly could.

CHAPTER 13

"You've seemed rather dull the last week, Lieutenant," Finch said over the rattle of the coach. "Are you already regretting the extension of your stay?"

Now he was. Harvey pasted on a smile. "I've simply been tired."

"I've been out of sorts since Madame d'Amilly's card party." Finch put his hands on his knees. "She is quite the extravagant woman."

Spending an excessive amount of money she didn't have and carrying on with Parisian gentlemen while her husband was in the country. Leaving her stepdaughter to try to establish her own future with no support from the ones who should be most concerned. "I cannot say I enjoyed her company."

Finch laughed. "You made a good show of it."

Had he? Harvey pursed his lips. He'd only been attempting to get the information Admiral Pratt wanted while keeping Madame d'Amilly away from Gabrielle and

Finch. He thought he'd been succeeding until he saw Gabrielle's face.

"You have the same expression you had a few days ago at church," Finch said. "Am I so dull?"

"Not at all, my friend." His mind was simply cluttered. Incredibly so. What he wouldn't give for a few days of a deck under his feet, the wind at his back, and the steady roll of an ocean. All the better if there were no land in sight. Conditions to clear his thoughts and make his life make sense.

As the coach turned, a domed building came into view at the end of the street. "Ah, there it is," Finch said. "Fortunately for you, we haven't far to go this morning." The building was blocked from view when the coach finished its turn, cutting off Harvey's study.

"What is it?"

"The Luxembourg Palace. You wished to see it, did you not?"

Harvey closed his eyes. He'd wanted Finch to see it with Gabrielle. "Of course I did. I wonder that you should have remembered."

Finch lifted a shoulder. "I thought it would be better than you wandering the Tuileries gardens again."

Again? Harvey folded his arms. He'd only walked there yesterday. And for less than an hour on Monday. Sunday he had stayed at the embassy. And Saturday was mostly spent trying to find an acquaintance of Admiral Pratt, so he was only at the Tuileries gardens for a very short amount of time. That was hardly excessive. One could have a favorite place in the city, could he not?

"Perhaps you will find the Luxembourg gardens to your liking and will take your walks there. I daresay they are not so crowded as the Tuileries."

That wasn't the point. The Tuileries were where he and Gabrielle met. He had some connection to that place. "I hear they are beautiful." But what gardens in Paris were not?

The coach let them out at the large wooden gate of the palace, and Harvey trudged down the steps. The sun poked out from behind the clouds, its glancing beams more concentrated than a usual sunny day. He squinted, taking in the palace and surrounding buildings in neat rows down the street. Carriages and citizens milled about on their respective journeys.

Finch stopped at the gatehouse, which was the domed building they'd seen from the carriage, and turned back toward the street as though waiting. Harvey paused beside him. "Shall we go in?"

"If you like. I am waiting for a couple of guests."

Had he invited the Borde family? They seemed to be his greatest friends in Paris. Though, now that he thought on it, he didn't think Finch had paid a visit since the card party. How strange. Perhaps the family had left Paris to pay a visit to friends. Or the seaside. Finch had returned looking forlorn. Somehow, according to Finch, they had reversed roles after Madame d'Amilly's party.

"Excellent, here they are." Finch rushed forward as a simple but elegant coach rolled to a stop. He opened the door and extended his hand to someone inside. Out stepped Madame Necker, and a little tension in Harvey's shoulders loosened. At least it was someone he knew and liked. The next was a young girl, about eight years of age, in a white frilly gown. That would be Anne-Louise, the Neckers' only child.

Harvey bowed when Madame Necker spotted him. This wouldn't be a terrible outing. He could stay with Anne-

Louise and point out the silly aspects of paintings while Finch crooned over every line and paint stroke. They would both enjoy themselves.

Finch reached into the carriage one more time, and the figure he guided out made Harvey freeze. Her hair, topped with a modest bergère hat, was not the dove shade she'd worn Thursday evening, but the rich brown he'd come to appreciate. She wore a red redingote that looked familiar, but fit better than the other clothes she'd worn when first they became acquainted. Had she taken to fixing up the rest of her ensembles?

Their gazes met, and for a moment the bustling world seemed to still around them. She looked well today. What's more, she did not look angry; she looked hopeful.

"Lieutenant Barlow." She curtsied. "How do you do?" she asked in English. She didn't emphasize her H sound as much as she had before. Finch must have practiced with her. Or she had practiced on her own.

"How do you do, Miss d'Amilly?" He returned her response in English.

"Very well, tank you." She held out her hand. He stared, remembering the feel of it Thursday night. He took her hand quickly, praying it did not seem too eager. With a bow, he hovered his face over her hand, but in the end he pulled away before his lips could brush her knuckles.

"Shall we continue into the palace?" Finch asked, assessing the group and then offering his arm to Madame Necker.

Wait. Finch was supposed to escort Gabrielle. As if reading his thoughts, she shrugged. "We have quite a lot of time," she whispered. "We can switch partners soon."

"It isn't that I do not like to be paired with you," Harvey

whispered. "It is only that the plan was..." He couldn't say it here in front of everyone.

"All in good time, Lieutenant." She slipped her arm through his without waiting for him to offer it and squeezed.

"Have I missed something?" Harvey asked. "Have you given up on him?"

She smiled, shaking her head. The curls around her neck swayed. "Heavens, no. Thursday evening went too well in that regard."

That's what he had thought, but her sadness following the event suggested otherwise. "What changed?" Harvey smoothed his fingers over hers. She gripped his arm in a confident hug.

"I came to a realization on some things." Her brow furrowed. "And more questions on others. But my frustrations about what happened have dissipated."

"I am a lucky man," he said and not in jest. He thought for certain that she would go silent toward him the rest of his stay in Paris. And as soon as he left, he would likely never see or hear from her again. Perhaps he would meet her in London as Mrs. Edward Finch. His body tightened like he'd been kicked in the stomach. He smoothed his waistcoat, attempting to regain a sense of indifferent calm. There was no reason to react to the thought of her as Finch's wife in such a way, but the ill sensation would not leave him quickly.

"Minette," Gabrielle called, motioning the girl over. Harvey had heard some of the *philosophes* call her that a few times at the last salon dinner they attended, but Gabrielle had never used it before. "Come walk with us."

He wanted to know more about what realizations she'd come to and what questions she now had. He wanted to apologize again for turning the card game into a battle of ideologies. Having young ears as company would make that difficult. He would have to practice some creativity.

The dark-haired girl gave Harvey a wary expression, but when he offered her his free arm she accepted his token of friendship. They proceeded through the gatehouse's two wooden doors, nearly twice as tall as he was, following after Finch and Madame Necker.

They paused in the salon just through the gates, and Madame Necker turned back. "Shall we begin with the Rubens gallery?"

Harvey and Gabrielle looked at each other, but she gave no indication that she had a preference of which gallery to start with.

"I cannot object to Rubens," Harvey said. They followed their leaders to the right, walking down a grand hall until they reached a gallery of massive paintings.

"These detail the life of Marie de' Medici," Finch said over his shoulder in his finest professor voice. Madame Necker seemed an excellent companion for him, speaking very little and acting suitably impressed by his knowledge. But Gabrielle needed to be there on his arm, hanging onto his every word.

She released his arm, but instead of making her way to Finch, she wandered toward the opposite side of the gallery, where Marie de' Medici's later life was depicted. Anne-Louise gave him a look that clearly read she did not appreciate being left with the foreign naval officer and scampered over to her mother. Abandoned, Harvey glanced between the two groups. There wasn't any question who he'd rather join and he hoped it wasn't terribly obvious when he strode to Gabrielle's side.

"What are you doing?" he asked softly.

"I am enjoying this painting," she said, waving a hand toward a canvas where two young women were surrounded by a troupe of Greek deities. "The Exchange of the Princesses."

"Ah." Harvey put his hands behind his back. "Yes, it is very lovely."

"Two girls leaving their countries for marriage."

No wonder she'd been drawn to it. "They seem to be welcomed by their new countries." At least most of the figures seemed pleased. There was one lamenting nymph or some such figure in the corner who did not seem happy with the proceedings.

"So it would seem." Gabrielle wandered slowly toward the next painting.

He hurried to catch up with her. "You do not sound convinced."

Gabrielle shrugged, looking back at the two princesses. "Did they understand the situation completely? Or did they rush in without thought?"

This was about her situation, not really about the sixteenth-century princesses. In reality, he didn't think they would have had much choice. "Perhaps not. Sometimes we see an opportunity and have to take it without much deliberation. It is how things work at sea. Sometimes you take the prize, sometimes you are the captured prize. But if you sit and wait until the perfect opportunity comes to you, you usually end up being the prize rather than the victor."

She tapped her rosy lips thoughtfully. "And I want to be the victor, certainly. But what if the prize you think you won turns out to not be what you thought?"

Harvey nodded. "That happens sometimes."

"What if you are left behind for long periods with no one to turn to?" She was turned toward the paintings, but it didn't appear that she was seeing them. Was she thinking of Finch being assigned to diplomatic missions when he could not bring her with him? That would be daunting in a country where you did not know the language or anyone around you.

"One would hope there would be a system of female relations who would be on the ready to offer support and companionship." Harvey smiled, trying to ease her fears. "In my family that is certainly the case. My sisters are very fond of new sisters-in-law, to the point of nearly forgetting the brother responsible for bringing said sister-in-law into the family even exists." He clamped his mouth shut. Did it sound like he was promoting his family? And in essence himself? In all actuality, his sisters would adore Gabrielle. Sophia would teach her English, Lydia would make it her quest to beat her at cards, and Violet would fill her ears with all the family stories. He smiled. It was a lovely picture, if he were being honest.

Gabrielle laughed. "I think I would like your sisters." Then she sobered. "I do not think Monsieur Finch has sisters."

Another point in favor of him. Harvey blinked. No, they were supposed to be finding points for Finch. Harvey wasn't looking for...

He watched Gabrielle continue down the gallery. Finch and Madame Necker had finished the one side and turned around to come back the other way, heading in her direction. Why was it easier to see her in Downham Cottage than Miss Pratt? She wanted simplicity rather than lavishness. Friendship rather than society. He wanted all those things as well, but most of all he wanted...her.

Everything rushed in at that moment as though a seawall had burst, picking him up and battering him against the rocky shore of realization. All this time he'd been helping pave the way for Finch to catch her, but now he did not want Finch to have her.

But *she* wanted Finch. She wanted his life in London. She wanted the safety and security of a husband who wouldn't be constantly at war. Good-natured, kind-hearted, eager-to-please Finch. He couldn't argue her choice when they'd worked so hard to get this far.

"Why is it you are staring at her?"

Harvey startled. Anne-Louise had appeared at his elbow as if out of nowhere. "Who am I staring at?"

"Mademoiselle d'Amilly."

"I was not staring at her." He turned his back on the other adults. "I was regarding the painting."

Anne-Louise folded her arms, and unconvinced frown on her face. "The one with all the flying babies?"

"Exactly so." Harvey copied her stance. "I thought it was quite..." Frivolous? Excessive?

"No, you weren't." Anne-Louise shrugged. "My *mère* says Mademoiselle d'Amilly is in love with you or Monsieur Finch. She isn't certain which."

Blast it all. "She certainly is not in love with me." The pace of his heart at the thought of being the object of her love belied his true desires. He had to admit a small part of him wished it were so. How could this match have gone so completely awry?

Monsieur Finch patted Gabrielle's hand as they walked through another gallery. "Some of the greatest masters are within these walls. His Majesty certainly has a fine collection of art."

"Yes, he certainly does." Why was Harvey hanging so far back from the rest of them? Ever since she rejoined Monsieur Finch and Madame Necker, he'd stayed aloof. Occasionally Anne-Louise would run back and whisper something to him, which he would shake his head at. The girl would then walk away with her chin held high, as though not satisfied with whatever he had told her. Very curious.

"This, I believe, is a da Vinci," Monsieur Finch said, pulling her toward a painting of Jean-Baptiste while Madame Necker hung back to look at something else. As they approached, another party of viewers crossed their path—a middle-aged gentleman and lady with two young women Gabrielle assumed to be their daughters.

Monsieur Finch nodded to the group. Then he froze, his arm going rigid. Before Gabrielle could ask him what was wrong, the older gentleman bowed. "Bonjour, Monsieur Finch. I trust you are well."

The ladies in his party stood still as statues. The mother and one of the girls practically gaped at Monsieur Finch, while the other looked everywhere except at him.

"I am well, thank you. Quite well." Monsieur Finch's voice had jumped up at least one octave. "Bonjour monsieur, madame, mesdemoiselles."

The ladies curtsied, mumbling their greeting, after which everyone stood unmoving and silent until Gabrielle started to squirm.

"Will you introduce us to your friend?" the gentleman asked.

"Oh, yes. Yes. This is..." Monsieur Finch looked at her, eyes wide with panic. Had he forgotten her name? "Mademoiselle d'Amilly." He practically shouted it. Her name echoed through the gallery.

What awkwardness had she stumbled upon? She'd known all along of Monsieur Finch's tendency toward causing embarrassment, but this was another matter entirely. The air between the two parties buzzed with something she could not name, but she wished to be free from it immediately. She beat down the urge to recoil and run off to Harvey like Anne-Louise had been doing.

She nudged Monsieur Finch. "Your friends?"

"Yes." Was he in pain? He sounded as though someone had stepped on his toe. "Allow me to introduce Monsieur and Madame Borde, and their daughters Mademoiselle Marie-Anne Françoise Borde..." He swallowed and cleared his throat. "...And Jacqueline."

Gabrielle curtsied. Still no one moved. She glanced around for Harvey. Where was he to save her from this?

"We were just about to—" she began.

"Might I speak with you a moment?" Monsieur Borde asked, motioning for Monsieur Finch to follow him. Gabrielle let go as fast as she could, lest he drag her into some other uncomfortable situation.

With the gentlemen gone, the ladies turned their full attention to her, even the daughter who had been seemingly disinterested before.

"Monsieur Finch has spoken so kindly of all of you," Gabrielle said. "It is an honor to finally make your acquaintance."

No response. Had they lost their ability to speak? They scrutinized her from head to toe until she wanted to melt into the floor. "Do you visit the Palais du Luxembourg often?" she asked.

"Yes," the mother said.

Nothing else.

Gabrielle nodded. "I have not been here in several years. I forgot how many masterpieces are here."

In the silence that followed, she scanned the gallery. Harvey stood in a corner with Anne-Louise arguing over something. Gabrielle wanted to run to him and hide behind his broad shoulders from whatever this bizarre interaction was. Monsieur Finch and Monsieur Borde stood at the end of the hall, the older man scratching his wigged head while Monsieur Finch stared at the floor. All of these uncomfortable encounters. This gallery was cursed.

There was only one thing to do. "I do hope you enjoy your visit to the gallery, madame. Mesdemoiselles," she added with a curtsy. "If you will excuse me." Thank the heavens Monsieur Finch would be returning to London and not in constant contact with this odd family. If she married him and they stayed in Paris, she would be forced to speak with them regularly. She could only hope they grew less awkward on better acquaintance.

Gabrielle walked casually toward Harvey, though she wanted to hurry. She pretended to notice the paintings and nodded at Madame Necker when she passed her.

"What does love mean, monsieur? You do not make sense." Anne-Louise jutted out her chin, as though daring the lieutenant to give her a bad answer.

Harvey ran a hand over his face. "Are you certain you have only eight years to your name?"

"You ignored my question." She folded her arms.

What on earth were they discussing? Gabrielle slowed her walk.

"There are many sorts of love, Mademoiselle Necker," he said.

Gabrielle halted. She turned toward a da Vinci portrait

of a woman in a red gown a few paintings away from them. The woman stared out of her canvas, as enthralled by this conversation as Gabrielle.

"And which do you have for her?" Anne-Louise asked.

"You know, when people are older they do not always like to discuss their feelings toward another person."

They hardly liked to discuss such things with themselves. Gabrielle held perfectly still, worried too loud a breath would make her miss something. Anne-Louise was trying to root out a confession of love from Harvey. Her heart pounded. She'd never considered that he could be in love. He'd never spoken of anyone, and at the card party he had insisted he did not seek it. But could there be someone he desired, deep down? Clearly he did not care for her to know.

"Yes, yes. Just like d'Alembert and Mademoiselle de Lespinasse do not discuss it," Anne-Louise huffed. "You will not answer my question."

"I...do not know the answer to your question."

"It is not so difficult to say yes, I love her, or no, I do not." The girl's young voice sounded almost amusing in this conversation. "Which is it?"

Gabrielle swiveled her head to watch him. *Yes, Harvey, which is it?* Was there an English girl who held his heart, waiting for him to return?

Harvey wagged a finger at Anne-Louise. "You are a very persuasive girl." He leaned in. "But I know how to be stubborn as well. I learned that, at least, in the navy."

Anne-Louise crossed her arms. "Then I will tell everyone that you are in love with Mademoiselle d'Amilly."

With her? Gabrielle clapped a hand to her mouth. That would spell disaster. Why, then, did it make her insides flutter?

"No!" Harvey glanced around to see if anyone was looking, and Gabrielle quickly snapped her head back to the woman in red. "No, no. That would do far more harm than good, mademoiselle. I sincerely hope you do not do that."

The Necker girl grunted. "Coward," she muttered. Then the sound of pattering feet crossed behind Gabrielle going down the hall. Had Élisabeth put something strange in the tea that morning? Gabrielle was not following most of what was going on since they entered this gallery.

She nearly said, "So you are a coward now," to Harvey, the need to pull him into a conversation insatiable. But he watched the little girl with pain creasing his face. She turned back to her new friend, the painting. She sensed so much internal turmoil in this room, but she couldn't understand what it all meant. As she watched Harvey, wishing she knew what was troubling him and wishing she could take the hurt away, she realized that in all the turmoil she sensed in the room, none rang louder than her own. And she couldn't, for all the world, take it out to examine it. If she did, she feared their plans would be irrevocably undone.

CHAPTER 14

Harvey sat in the ambassador's box at the Palais-Royal, watching Finch play the perfect beau to the woman he loved. The spot between his eyebrows had grown tight and sore since the ambassador's party had descended on the loge. From his seat behind Finch and Gabrielle he saw every whisper, every shared laugh, every demure smile, and he regretted for the hundredth time his plans to stay longer.

Patrons throughout the opera house were taking their seats, talking excitedly about the opening of the production and its famous composer. All of Paris seemed to be there, including the young *dauphine* and *dauphin*. Marie-Antoinette, only eighteen years old, drew many whispers and stares in the direction of the royals' private loge. As she reacted, so would the rest of them be forced to react. How strange a world courts were. Harvey distracted himself from the romance blossoming in front of him with wondering about the *dauphin*'s future reign. The king was still in good health, but the prince could very well find himself on the throne in not many years.

The Neckers and Lord Stormont discussed something from one of the *philosophes*' letters, which Harvey found difficult to follow. When he'd exhausted watching the royalty and examining the stone cherubim encircling the stage, his eyes fell on Gabrielle's hair. She'd powdered it brown tonight, and it was all he could do to keep himself from reaching out to touch the soft curl that hung down the back of her neck. She wore the blue gown, the same one she'd worn that first night they'd attended the Neckers' salon. How far she'd come since that timid descent down the stairs in her stepmother's ill-fitting clothes. Wariness had been replaced by confidence and conversation. The more time he spent in her presence, the more he hated Finch. He should have offered to marry her that day at Stohrer's. Never mind his promotion or his talks with Admiral Pratt.

The curtain rose, and conversations hushed. The orchestra began a stately and mournful tune as a singer dressed as an ancient soldier walked forward on the stage and collected two birdlike objects from the ground. Harvey planted his elbow on the arm of his chair and rested his face against his fist. He'd forgotten these things had so little words sometimes.

Try as he might, he could not block out Finch and Gabrielle's conversation. A king figure arrived on the stage, but still no words were sung to keep Harvey's attention from straying to the way the pale blue silk of her gown draped down Gabrielle's back.

"I am so glad to have someone to sit with for this performance," Finch whispered.

"Lord Stormont was most kind to invite me." She kept her head pointed toward the stage, whereas Finch seemed to watch her more than the people moving grandly about the stage to the orchestra's strains. In this one thing, Harvey could not blame him.

"Lieutenant Barlow and I insisted you be among our party."

Harvey winced. He had insisted at first, back before Finch had a change of heart regarding Gabrielle. The more he watched Finch angling toward Gabrielle, the more he wished he hadn't agreed to help her catch his eye.

Two female figures drifted across the stage. Then the king began to sing. Finally. He mourned the need to sacrifice his daughter for the fortune of his fleet, and Harvey fidgeted in his seat. Sacrificing a daughter for a navy hit a little too true. Admiral Pratt wasn't really sacrificing his daughter. Marriage was not death. But it was a match neither he nor Miss Pratt would have chosen for themselves had it not been key to pushing his advancement. Guilt tugged at Harvey's consciousness. He'd dreaded Miss Pratt's indifference toward him, but was he really the one to blame, agreeing to a match she did not want?

He rubbed his brow. It served him right. How many times had his father told him that love was not part of marriage decisions? He'd tried to keep himself free from it. Of course, he hadn't anticipated love hitting him with the full force of his arrow at point-blank range. This journey should not have allowed him time to fall.

"I return to London in a couple of months for a brief stay," Finch said softly as the opera's king sang on. "I had hoped to bring someone with me." Gabrielle's head snapped toward him.

Harvey set his jaw. That was it—the phrase they'd been working for all these weeks. Gabrielle's passage out of France and the clutches of her stepmother. He should have exulted. Instead, the phrase knifed at his gut.

"Perhaps you shall," Gabrielle said, slow and steady. How was she so calm? Not even a smile graced her rouged lips.

Finch took a deep breath, then nodded. "Perhaps I shall."

Harvey sat back as the conversation fell to silence. That was it. His task was finished. He'd set out to make Gabrielle a match. He needn't torture himself anymore. Finch and Gabrielle could carry their courtship on their own shoulders from here.

As the act progressed, Gabrielle took out her fan, beating it rapidly against the heat of the packed opera house. Harvey wished he'd thought to bring one, but as a navy man he tended to be constantly out of the habit. They'd been taught how to fire big guns and chart their location by the stars when he was younger, not how to survive overheated theatres while listening to the object of your desires flirt with another.

He had to keep reminding himself he'd chosen this path. Try as he might, he could not escape his own shortsightedness. Taking his father's advice, his admiral's advice, had plunged him into a situation he would long regret.

Before the second act finished, Gabrielle could not stand it any longer. This growing illness in the pit of her stomach since Monsieur Finch mentioned bringing her back to London made it impossible to sit still in a crowded loge. Her chest constricted painfully. She needed air and a moment alone or she would faint like those prideful girls at balls who had laced their stays too tight and pretended that was always how they looked.

"I'm sorry," she whispered in Monsieur Finch's direction. "I need some air." She rose swiftly, wishing she and Finch had not sat in the front row of seats in the loge. Everyone in the ambassador's party would see her leave.

She kept her head turned away as she hurried past the other chairs, not wanting to see Harvey's face. A hand caught hers, gentle but strong enough she could not get away without making a scene, and her heart missed a beat.

"Are you well?" Harvey asked.

"Yes, I will only be a moment." She tugged her hand free, and he let her go. His warmth seared into her hand, and a realization she had tried so hard to ignore the last couple of weeks pounded at her temples. She rushed down the opera theatre's grand staircase and through the massive corridors of the Palais-Royal, trying not to run and draw further attention.

She burst out the doors into the gardens. Lanterns lit the stately lines of vegetation, but few people walked the gardens with the opera in progress. She made for the greenery. There was nothing quite like nature to clear one's mind. Would it calm her racing pulse?

Only in the safety of a row of trees did she slow her pace. She released her skirts, which she hadn't realized she was clutching as though her safety depended upon it. The click of her shoes on the paved path slowed the storm that had risen inside her, but it did not silence it. She laid a hand on her face, which felt hot after her exit.

This wasn't how her plan was supposed to happen!

She retrieved her fan from her pocket and waved it despite the chill evening. Calm. She needed calm. How could she reason what to do with these feelings—feelings toward the man who was her accomplice, not her goal—when she could not settle her nerves? She swallowed, slowly stilling her fan. Love. She did love him, didn't she?

Gabrielle hugged herself tightly as she walked. No stars shone overhead, and a breeze picked up that she hadn't noticed before. Darkness loomed in the stretches between the meager lanterns. She needed to love Monsieur Finch. He was her best chance. He was kind and flattering and odd in an amusing way. But her mind would not rest in thoughts of him. Always the memories of Harvey peeked out in places she least expected them. His teasing smile, his generosity, his encouragement. Not to mention the way his square jaw tightened when he was trying not to laugh.

She buried her face in her hand. Why had she let it come to this? Did she not care about impending war? About loneliness in a country she didn't know? How would marrying Harvey put her in a better situation than what she was currently in?

Laughter from farther down the lane stopped her short. She did not want to interact with anyone while sifting through these thoughts. She scanned the gardens. A wall of the Palais-Royal stood not far away. She ducked through the trees to reach it. The lantern light didn't touch here. She leaned her back against the wall, its stone cold through the silk of her gown.

Marriage to Harvey had its attractions. Financial security. Respect in Society. A cottage in the country. Sisters! She closed her eyes, imagining. It was everything she could ever want in a situation.

But Harvey doesn't love you. In the quiet of the gardens, the thought screamed in her ears. Would he not have told her by now if he had? Their quest would have been much simpler if he had offered for her hand instead of having to catch a rather oblivious man's eye. Something had held him back.

She played with one of her curls. Of course there was how he spoke to her. Surely there was something in that. He was a friendly soul, even to her stepmother, but sometimes it felt like more. His flirtation, his teasing. She dropped the curl and straightened. If she changed her target, turned her attention to Harvey... No. How ridiculous. He would see straight through her after helping her all this time. And he was to leave in little more than a week. She didn't have time.

Gabrielle let her arms fall to her sides. She sighed, tilting her head back to rest against the wall. She should just find happiness in what she had, not seek it in unattainable places. Her eyes burned, and she brushed at them impatiently. It would do her no good to cry.

"What is troubling you?"

She startled and pushed herself away from the wall. Harvey stood a few paces away, the faint lantern glow catching in his light brown hair. She wanted to run to him, to be encircled by his arms and held so long the fear and anguish melted away.

"Nothing. I am not troubled."

"You are not very good at lying."

"I am telling the—" A drop splattered against her nose.

Harvey looked toward the sky. A few cries erupted throughout the garden, and shadows ran for the palace as the rain increased. He took Gabrielle's hand. "Hurry. You'll ruin your gown." He pulled her toward one of the archways. Just beyond was a cloister lit with torches.

"There are already spots on it," she said as they reached the arch's shelter. She peeked around the edge of the arch.

It didn't appear anyone else had sought shelter in this walkway. "It is an old gown anyway."

"I like that gown."

Her stomach did a hopeful flip even as she tried to squash any yearning. "It's old and not the latest fashion."

He regarded her, and she wondered what he saw in the dim light. A friend? One whose company he had enjoyed for a time, but who he would likely not see again for a very long time, if ever. She clasped her hands, squeezing tightly against the aching in her heart.

"You wore it to the first salon we attended together. I'll always remember..." He shook his head, looking out into the rain.

"We don't have much longer together, do we?" The question slipped from her mouth, nearly drowned by the pattering of the storm.

"I don't like that thought."

He didn't? "Why not?" She drifted closer to him. This was going to hurt, when all her hope came crashing down around her.

"I'll miss our scheming."

Gabrielle laughed. They had done a good amount of that since they met.

"I'll miss finding pins and needles on the floor for you."

She attempted a pout, but it wasn't a very good one. "Are you poking fun at my distress?"

"I'll miss hearing you call me 'Arvey."

"*Coquin!*" She swatted at his arm. Making fun of her English. The rascal.

He snatched her hand and wrapped her arm around his. "I'll miss the fire in your eyes when you stand up for yourself." He finally met her gaze. The earthy scent of rain hovering over the gardens and cloister brought out the cedar and rosemary of his cologne. Was this a taste of the sweetness of his little Sussex cottage? It would haunt her the rest of her days.

"Harvey," she said, making sure she pronounced the H, "there was one option we did not consider." What was she saying? Her heart leapt to her throat.

He angled his body toward her. "In trying to catch Finch's eye?"

"No, I mean someone we did not consider." *Just say it, Gabrielle*.

His eyes narrowed. "Another of Stormont's clerks?"

She shook her head sharply. How could she say it? Once it was said, there was no returning. "Someone else who could take me away from here. Someone like..." She tightened her hold on his arm. Heat rose to her face, and she prayed he could not see it.

He stared into her eyes as her unfinished sentence hung between them. His chest rose and fell heavily. He took both of her hands in his, pulling her close. "Gabrielle..." He murmured something in English that she couldn't understand.

She rose up on her toes, his hands steadying her. "Please," she said in English. It sounded so desperate, but she was. She didn't want to think of Paris without Harvey. It had turned from a prison to a garden, one full of sweetness and laughter and light. His breath warmed her skin, pushing away the damp of the storm. His eyes were pinched in worry, but something else glimmered in their depths.

Gabrielle couldn't tell who closed the distance, but suddenly his lips were on hers. Fire shot through her veins, filling every part of her with light. He cupped her cheek with one hand, and she leaned into its safety and strength.

For a moment, all her worries melted into the rainy Paris night until all that existed was Harvey kissing her in the seclusion of the archway. For the briefest of moments, she had found heaven.

"Barlow?"

Gabrielle's eyes flew open.

"Barlow, is that you?"

She pulled away from Harvey, backing up until she hit the side of the arch. He looked ill. They both recognized the chipper voice.

Harvey stepped into the cloister and raised a hand. "I'm here, Finch."

"Did you find her? Is she well?"

She covered her mouth. No, she most certainly was not well. Kissing Harvey for all the world to see in the Jardins du Palais-Royal, and then getting interrupted by the man for whom she was supposed to learn to have feelings.

Monsieur Finch appeared in their archway. "Mademoiselle! You gave us all quite the fright. Madame Necker has been so worried."

"I apologize," Gabrielle said. "The theatre was too hot. It felt so wonderful out here."

"You are quite right." Monsieur Finch beamed.

Harvey stood as though his shoes had been nailed to the ground. Was he regretting what they'd done? Neither of them had spoken in specific agreement of what Gabrielle had proposed.

Proposed. *Ciel*, she'd practically proposed to him, hadn't she? And he hadn't accepted. Something held him back. He'd been trying to tell her before their kiss. A thousand possibilities drummed through her head.

"I will inform the Neckers that their charge has been located," Harvey said, backing into the cloister.

"It is the *entr'acte*," Monsieur Finch said. "You might find them in Madame d'Épiany's loge."

Harvey nodded, refusing to look at her. "I shall meet you shortly."

She wanted to reach out for him, tell him not to go. But Monsieur Finch's eager expression aimed at her kept her locked in place. She should not have tried to catch him. She should have waited and let an opportunity for marriage to a good man come upon her, rather than trying to force it. Anything she touched, any scheme she had, was always ruined by her attempt to control her destiny.

Harvey departed, finally looking back, his face unreadable.

"Are you certain you are well, mademoiselle?" Monsieur Finch asked. "You seem rather out of sorts. Was the opera too much for you?"

"Not at all." Harvey made it to the end of the walkway and turned so that her view of him was now obscured.

"I told you we would need that umbrella I brought. Did I not?" Monsieur Finch extended his arm to her.

"You certainly did." She took his arm, wishing it were Harvey's. Guilt flared, but she couldn't deny it. What was Harvey thinking right now? Was he regretting what they'd shared? Was he thinking about what she'd said? Arriving on the embassy doorstep asking after Monsieur Finch was no longer the most forward thing she'd ever done. A lady didn't confess her soul to a gentleman whose intentions she did not know.

"Lieutenant Barlow mentioned the chance of rain," Monsieur Finch said.

"He is a man of the navy. He understands the weather better than most of us." And a great many other things.

"He is a catch, to be certain," her companion said with a sigh. "The lieutenant is the luckiest of men."

Gabrielle narrowed her eyes, willing her face not to reveal her thoughts. "Why do you think so?"

Monsieur Finch smiled. "He has the loveliest little cottage in the country, so I am told. He is near to making post-captain. And, just between us..." He put a finger to his lips. "He is engaged to a lovely girl."

Gabrielle's mouth went dry. The sound of rain and the torchlights faded as her brain tried to make sense of what he had said. Surely he'd used the wrong phrase. Perhaps he had translated what he wanted to say incorrectly. Harvey wasn't engaged. He would have told her.

"Engaged?" she said, voice taut. "Is that what you said?"

Monsieur Finch nodded enthusiastically. "Isn't it wonderful? He's a good man, and I envy his happiness."

She still could not make sense of what he was saying. "Harvey Barlow is engaged? The lieutenant?" She had been correct. There was an English girl waiting for him. Another secret. Another thing he should have mentioned.

"Yes, our dear friend." He motioned in the direction Harvey had gone. "She's the daughter of an admiral, if I remember correctly. A fine match. I am very happy for him."

"Yes." Bile rose in her throat. Engaged to an admiral's daughter. And here she stood baring her soul while he was attempting to distance himself.

"If you will pardon my boldness, there is something I wish to ask you."

Her stomach clenched, and she threw her arm over it. "*Je vous prie de m'excuse,* monsieur. I think I am ill."

Monsieur Finch's eyes widened. "Oh, dear. Allow me to escort you home."

"No, I..." She couldn't imagine a ride in a carriage with him just now.

"You are in no state to return home on your own. I will find someone to inform the ambassador I've taken you back." He led them toward the doors of the Palais-Royal. "I am so sorry."

So was she. So very, very sorry.

Harvey raced down the grand staircase of the Palais-Royal. Gabrielle had been well a moment before Finch's interruption. More than well. She had been soft and sweet and sincere. Everything he'd been dreaming of for the last few weeks. His entire life, if he were being truly honest. Someone to prove his father wrong—that a relationship between two people could be more than just a business contract.

He nearly bowled a gentleman over at the bottom of the stairs and mumbled his apologies as he hurried on his way. He should be the one taking her home. They needed to talk about what happened and the complications it would cause. Miss Pratt, the admiral, the very real possibility he would be forced to leave. But if she really was ill, perhaps this wasn't the time. He made it to the doors that led out to the street. A footman opened one to let him through. He would speak with her tomorrow. Perhaps he could convince Madame d'Épinay to allow them to use her library again.

The rain had stopped, leaving the street a shimmering gray. His eyes took a moment to adjust after the brilliance of the Palais-Royal's foyer. There they were, off to the side and down a few steps.

"Would you not prefer to wait inside?" Finch asked her. "It might get too cold for you."

Gabrielle shook her head. She stood with arms crossed, staring down the road.

"At least take my coat."

"I'm not cold, but thank you."

Harvey hurried to them, and Finch turned. "Ah, Barlow. We are awaiting the coach. I should have brought my umbrella out with me. I left it by my chair."

"I will stay with her while you fetch it," Harvey said quickly. "We wouldn't want her to be rained on while she's ill."

"Oh, thank you. You are quite right." Finch clapped him on the shoulder. "I'll be back in a moment, mademoiselle." He scurried away.

Gabrielle did not turn. Harvey took her arm. She was rigid. "Gabrielle, what is it?"

She whirled on him, breaking his hold. "You are engaged?"

Harvey took a step back. How had she heard about that? Only Stormont knew. His first morning in Paris came screeching back into his mind. The walk in the Tuileries. Blast it. He'd told Finch. He swiped a hand down his face. There was no denying it. She didn't deserve to be lied to.

"Not yet," he said, "but I very soon will be." Miss Pratt would have told all of London by now. If he withdrew his offer, she'd be ruined. Humiliated at the very least. Not to mention his naval career would be in tatters. He'd be doomed to command a guard ship at one of the dockyards or something far from war and prizes that could advance his career.

"You were practically engaged and still kissed me?"

She'd lowered her voice, but it still hit with the force of a broadside.

"I didn't mean to. It just happened." Had *he* been the instigator? His mind was muddled, but he could have sworn she'd started it.

"You let the moment carry you away," she said bitterly.

"No." He walked around her, forcing her to face him. "I care for you, Gabrielle. I truly do." More than he'd cared for anyone outside his family. If he could erase all the messy pieces of his life, he would make her part of that circle in a heartbeat. He stepped toward her.

"Stop!" She threw her arms out in front of her, her fists planted squarely on his chest. "Do not say that."

"But it's true." More than true. He *loved* her. But he couldn't say that right now. It would only make things worse.

She drew her hands back. "For far too long I have allowed myself to be hurt by those I once trusted. I will not let you hurt me as well."

A chill swept through Harvey. Her words echoed in his ears, hammered in his chest. He'd hurt her. He hadn't been trying to. He'd been trying to help. But he had all the same.

"I apologize, mademoiselle." How had it come to this? He should have known from the first day he wouldn't be able to resist her.

"Here it is!" came the cheerful voice that would haunt Harvey's dreams for the rest of his life. Finch appeared at the top of the stairs, waving his umbrella. "Wonderful invention, these."

"I bid you both goodnight." Harvey bowed to them and launched himself back up the steps. There was nowhere to go except back to the theatre and watch as a true hero saved Iphigénie from her parents' wicked doings or return to the gardens where he'd let his foolish hope get the best of him. At least in the theatre he could listen to the music without focusing on trying to understand the French lyrics and miss most of the story. In the gardens Gabrielle's memory would be there at every turn, trailing her orange blossom scent.

Harvey raked a hand through his hair, silently cursing. This was why his father had warned him against marrying for anything other than business. It hurt too much when everything fell apart.

CHAPTER 15

Harvey passed the dining room where the ambassador's party was eating their breakfast with their newspapers in the usual fashion. They wouldn't notice him sneak out. He walked quietly through the foyer to keep his shoes from echoing. He'd found ways to occupy himself throughout the city in the last week since the opera, mostly occupying the Tuileries Palace gardens.

"Barlow?"

He paused. Dash it all.

Lord Stormont popped his head into the foyer from the salon near the door. "Off on another walk through the city?"

Had he been so obvious? "I plan to enjoy every last minute I have in Paris."

"I would not enjoy myself wading through city streets day after day, but to each his own."

Harvey opened his mouth to respond but couldn't find the words. Stormont had caught him. He'd tried not to draw attention to the cloud that had encircled him after his admission to Gabrielle. The days between meetings before the opera had been dull, but these days without her, knowing he very well might not see her again, were something he could not describe. It was like drifting at sea without mast or sail or oar, longing to reach a far off shore but knowing he'd never make it. He'd made his decision and so had she.

"The king has taken ill," Stormont said gravely.

"George?"

"No, Louis." Stormont leaned against the doorframe. "The *dauphin* and *dauphine* were sent away."

"That sounds serious." The king was only sixty, maybe a little more.

The ambassador nodded. "It was a precaution, and they hope he will recover due to the fact he has had smallpox previously. But one can never guess with these sorts of things."

Harvey nodded solemnly. What would this mean for France's relationship with the colonies? A new king with a new circle of advisors. It was anyone's guess who would win as politicians jockeyed for position.

"Perhaps you should write to the admiral," Stormont said. "He might ask you to extend your stay."

Extend again? That was the last thing he wanted to do. "You are quite right. I shall delay my walk." Harvey turned around to return upstairs to his room.

"Barlow?"

He paused.

"Are you on the path you truly want to be?"

Harvey swallowed. "I believe so. Yes." He tried to muster lightheartedness. Lord Stormont's face read that he didn't believe it.

"It's a good question to consider at every stage of our

lives," the ambassador said. "I will leave you to it." He disappeared back into the salon, and Harvey hurried to his room in case the man chased him down to bring up some other uncomfortable subject.

He took out paper and ink and set them on his desk. The ambassador's question poked at him, refusing to leave. His career depended on this path. Admiral Pratt had done so much for him as a captain, pushing for him to be made a lieutenant before the end of the war despite his youth to prevent him getting stuck with little pay and few options for advancement. The admiral had placed him on ships despite the difficulty of finding positions. Marrying the man's daughter didn't seem unreasonable, and it would help him advance as well. They wouldn't deny an admiral's request to promote his son-in-law. This *was* the path he wanted.

The paper sat before him, ready to be filled with the news, but Harvey couldn't bring himself to pick up the pen. The longer it rested on his desk, the less he wanted to write this letter. He tried desperately to hold onto what he knew he wanted. What he knew he should want. But still the page stared back at him, empty and lifeless.

Angry voices billowed from the salon as Gabrielle trudged downstairs. One of them was a deep, masculine tone. Père? He'd been in the country for months. She hurried the last few steps and darted into the room.

Her father and stepmother stood at one end. Before she could express her joy at seeing him, both rounded on her, Père's eyes dark and dangerous, Élisabeth's wide and livid.

Gabrielle halted, uncertain if they were angry with each other and she'd interrupted, or if they were angry at her.

"I'll return later," she mumbled, backing away.

"What have you done, you *garce*?" Élisabeth shouted.

Gooseflesh shot across Gabrielle's skin. "What do you mean?"

"Yesterday evening, Madame Garnier told me she saw you at the opera last week out in the gardens with a man. Kissing that man."

Gabrielle's blood ran cold. How had anyone seen them? Everyone had returned inside.

Élisabeth put a hand on her waist. "What's more, it was one of those *anglais* who work for the ambassador." The woman raised a finger. "I knew those foreigners were trouble. I should not have allowed you to bring them here, parading them around right under my nose while you had ill intentions."

"I did not have ill intentions." Gabrielle looked to her father for support, but his cold gaze repelled her plea.

"I find that difficult to believe when you were hiding the man in your room before the card party."

Gabrielle shrank back. Of course Élisabeth had spied him. Why had she not said anything? Most likely she'd saved it on purpose to use against her. The hypocrite. "You entertain gentlemen at your *toilette*. How is it wrong when I do the same?"

"You are not married, Gabrielle." Élisabeth clicked her tongue, as if marriage made the situation any different. "Though you would have been shortly if you hadn't ruined everything. We have been discussing marriage plans with the family Longueville."

"Marriage?" Gabrielle blurted. They hadn't thought to consult her? Or even inform her? She'd assumed her stepmother's comment about paying Monsieur Longueville attention had been wishful thinking.

"Yes," her father said. Once this man had been all that was warm and good in her life. Élisabeth had poisoned him, leaving a cold shell of who her father had once been. "And now the man refuses. The rumors are all over Paris, Gabrielle."

There were rumors all over Paris about Monsieur Goncourt and about her stepmother. Why did that matter? But the thought of everyone talking about her in hushed tones made her insides quiver.

"We must make him," Élisabeth said. "We cannot afford not to."

A knock sounded at the door. Gabrielle sent a prayer of relief heavenward. A moment of reprieve. She'd flee when her stepmothers' friends arrived.

The footman opened the door and a moment later presented Monsieur Finch into the salon. Gabrielle stared, unsure if she wanted to laugh or cry. He carried a little bouquet of lily of the valley, the tiny white blossom trembling as he walked.

"*Bonjour*, mademoiselle, madame, monsieur." He bowed to each.

"It's you!" Élisabeth stalked over to him like a rising storm.

Monsieur Finch shuffled back. "Pardon me. What?"

"You were the one compromising our daughter at the opera. Kissing her for the world to see."

Ciel. They thought she'd kissed Monsieur Finch. Gabrielle swept the memories of the kiss with Harvey out of her mind as she stepped forward. She couldn't allow this false accusation and couldn't allow her tender feelings about the real event to interfere. "No, no, that isn't what happened."

"You compromised her honor, and now there are rumors that the both of you are engaged," Élisabeth shrieked. "Engaged! To a penniless Englishman like you? Ridiculous."

"I am not *penniless*." Monsieur Finch retreated toward the door, holding the flowers before him like a shield.

"What are we to do with her now? You've ruined her for Monsieur Longueville."

Gabrielle ground her teeth. Monsieur Finch may not be the man of her dreams, but he was a kind soul who did not deserve this reproach. She threw herself between her stepmother and Monsieur Finch. "How dare you."

Élisabeth pulled up short.

Gabrielle couldn't contain it any longer. The anger burst out uncontrolled. "How dare you accuse us of indiscretion after your own liaisons." Élisabeth's face went red. Her father looked away. "I have been more tainted by your reputation than by the time spent with Monsieur Finch. What's more, it wasn't Monsieur Finch—"

"You ungrateful vermin!" Élisabeth snarled. "You'll be thrown out into the gutter."

"So be it." She'd taken this woman's criticism for too long. In her mind she could almost see Harvey smiling. For the first time in more than a week, it gave her strength rather than anger and hurt. "I will not allow you to speak in this manner to my friend."

"You will leave this house immediately." Her stepmother shot forward, arm raised to slap Gabrielle. Before Gabrielle could flinch, a hand snatched her arm and swung her out of the way. Monsieur Finch tucked her behind him.

"We are engaged," Monsieur Finch said.

Everyone in the room froze. What was he doing? She couldn't see his face. Those three words should have brought elation, but she felt hollow.

"That is why we were seen together at the opera," he said. Was there a tightness in his voice? "Mademoiselle d'Amilly is undeserving of this censure or this gossip."

He was standing up for her. A lump formed in her throat at the bravery she hadn't expected from him. To commit to something as serious as an engagement...

"I knew it," Élisabeth hissed. She turned to Père. "You see? You see the daughter you have cursed us with?"

Père did not respond.

"Engaged to an Englishman." She threw up her hands. "Well, we do not approve of this match. You will not be allowed to wed."

Monsieur Finch spoke calmly. "We will wed in England. In our country she is of age where parental consent is not necessary."

"You would leave France and everything you know behind?" Père asked. Though indignation tainted his voice, Gabrielle thought she heard a little hurt as well. It pulled at her heart. But she had to take this chance. She'd been working for it. Just as Harvey had worked for his chance. Her throat tightened. He was taking care of himself, and now she would do the same.

Gabrielle lifted her chin. "I need a place where I can be safe and wanted," she said. "One that is free from ridicule and gossip and financial uncertainty. I cannot find that here." Père flinched like she'd struck him. Could he even comprehend how much siding with Élisabeth in this matter pained Gabrielle? The man she'd adored as a child was nowhere to be found anymore.

"Pack your things, then," Élisabeth said evenly, crossing

her arms. "And do not dare take anything of mine with you." The look on her face read she didn't believe Gabrielle had the audacity to do it. "I cannot believe you would marry a clerk. You little fool."

"You married a farmer and tried to style him as a noble," Gabrielle said. "Then you ruined him financially and in the eyes of Society. Who is the fool?" She turned on her heel and strode from the room without looking back.

CHAPTER 16

"*Naturellement*, you may stay here," Madame d'Épinay cried, setting down her teacup. "What a horrible hypocrite of a woman, kicking you out of their home."

Gabrielle nodded. The skin of her face felt dry and taut after the tears shed during her hasty departure. She hated that she cried. It only gave Élisabeth more reason to gloat as she examined Gabrielle's trunks for the clothing that was "rightfully" hers. She hadn't let Gabrielle keep anything, even if it had been altered. Those dresses would be sold for pin money.

Père had been achingly absent from the proceedings. He'd been readying to retreat back to the country manor, leaving Gabrielle to face the jackal that was his wife alone.

Monsieur Finch sat beside her on the salon sofa, straight as a lamppost. He'd hardly spoken to her since his declaration to her parents. He held his teacup but did not drink.

"But you are engaged, then?" Madame d'Épinay said. "I thought…well, that doesn't matter. This is happy news."

Gabrielle glanced at Monsieur Finch, who nodded with a forced smile. "We are very happy."

Only they weren't. They had hardly spoken on the carriage ride to Madame d'Épinay's. Gabrielle couldn't decide if he looked depressed or resigned. It wasn't the reaction she'd hoped to elicit upon becoming engaged.

"I will have your things taken upstairs," Madame d'Épinay said, rising. "And I will have your room prepared. You may stay as long as you need, of course."

"Merci, madame," Gabrielle said as the woman left. She guessed correctly that the *saloniste* would help them, and she was grateful she had somewhere familiar to go. Silence prevailed for a moment, letting in the hum of the streets and the creaking of floorboards overhead as someone moved about. Finally she turned to him. "I appreciate all you have done for me today, monsieur. You are a good man to sacrifice so much. However, I feel as though perhaps you might regret your decision. We do not have to go through with this."

He set his untouched tea aside. "After all that has happened? What would you do? You cannot go back to that place."

No, she couldn't. Not for some time, if ever. "I will think of something."

He shook his head. "I will not leave you to your own devices. If my behavior the night of the opera hurt your reputation, I cannot leave you alone."

"It might not have been you."

He held up his hands. "Both Lieutenant Barlow and I contributed to it in some way, I am certain."

Gabrielle wrung her hands. Harvey had much larger of a contribution.

"Do you wish to remain in Paris?" he asked.

She shook her head. She'd wanted this so badly. Why, now that it was coming to life before her eyes, did she feel sick? Harvey was not an option. He could not save her from this.

"Then it is settled. I will speak with Madame d'Épinay about your staying until June. It's only a month away. And I will write to my mother about finding someone for you to stay with in London until we are...wed." He gulped.

A lump formed in her throat. She didn't deserve Monsieur Finch's generosity, not when she was pining for another. But someday that would fade. They could find love and happiness.

"Thank you for your kindness." She had to tell him what had happened at the Palais-Royal. But he'd already turned away, apparently lost in thought. There would be time for her admission when the dust of this morning settled. Then he could choose for himself if he wanted to leave. The uncertainty stretching before her made it hard to breathe. What would happen tomorrow, next week, in a month? Where would she be next year? A great curtain hung between her and her future, and she could not see through it nor reach to pull it back. And deep down, there was only one person she wished would be behind it, but he was the only one she knew for sure wouldn't be—Harvey.

Barlow,

Yes, you certainly must stay until the king recovers or the worst happens. Send word the moment you hear any news. Such an upheaval in leadership could have widespread consequences where we are concerned.

A MATCH GONE AWRY

I have just received your report. Support for the Americans seems to be growing among the French. It's all bitterness, to be sure. Think of the repercussions should the colonies succeed in standing up to king and country? If France thinks she will not lose her colonies or worse, she is an imbecile.

Eugenia is in London again. She gets rather distracted with friends and acquaintances, of course, but I have no doubt she will be quite happy to see you and finalize the marriage contract. When the king is on the mend or has quit this mortal world, I bid you return as swiftly as you are able for both our sakes. The Admiralty is already outfitting additional ships for the blockade of Boston Harbour. If we do not move quickly with all our plans, we will lose our moment.

Godspeed,
Admiral Pratt

Harvey waited at Café de la Régence, scanning the patrons for Rouvroy. This was the coffeehouse the man said he frequented. He had the correct time and day. Now where was the sour creature?

The table shook as a patron walked past, rippling the surface of his coffee. He should have asked for more sugar or something sweet to dip into it, but he hadn't the stomach for sweet things the last two weeks. Parisian pastries reminded him of Gabrielle, and he needed to not think of that young lady. His heart took up its familiar ache. Confound it. He'd done well the last day or so. He tried to drown the feeling in a drink of his bitter coffee.

The door opened, and Harvey kept his eyes on his drink so the outside light wouldn't blind him. When the door shut again, he glanced up. A finely dressed gentleman with a marked sneer and gold-topped walking stick paraded through the tables.

At last. Harvey shot to his feet. Rouvroy glanced at him, frown deepening.

"*Bonjour*, Monsieur Rouvroy," Harvey said, nodding. "It is good to see you again."

"Lieutenant Barlow." He offered the barest of bows.

"Will you sit down?" Harvey indicated the chair across from him.

Rouvroy scanned the coffeehouse as though looking for someone. He must not have found him because he took the proffered chair with a huff. Harvey joined him. "Come to cross swords over the colonies again?" the man asked.

"Is there more to say?"

Rouvroy inclined his head. "Not very much." He waved down a server for a cup of coffee, then added to it from a flask.

"The colonies seem to have been forgotten for now," Harvey said. "The king's illness is on everyone's mind." He attempted to keep his tone disinterested.

"We shall see how that ends." Rouvroy took a long drink. "Manpeou says the archbishop has been summoned. His immunity did not protect him, it would seem."

"The archbishop?" He would only be summoned for last rites. That sounded serious indeed. Harvey might be on his way back to England very soon.

"Rumor has it the king looks terrible. Eruptions all over his skin." Rouvroy waved his hand around his face, nose wrinkled. "Terrible business."

"I do not envy him. I take it the family will not get to say goodbye."

"No, of course not. They cannot endanger the future

king. Only Madame du Barry is left." Rouvroy looked around the tables again. Apparently none of his friends had arrived yet. "I hear congratulations are in order for your friend." A wicked grin split his face.

Harvey pulled his brows together. "My friend?"

Rouvroy gestured impatiently. "The short one with whom we played *triomphe*."

"Finch?" He hadn't seen Finch much the last couple of weeks. Harvey had mostly dined in cafés or in his room after returning to the embassy after dinner each night. He'd only seen Finch passing through the corridors. The couple of times he had eaten dinner with the other diplomats, Finch had dined with friends at Madame d'Épinay's. "What congratulations?"

"He is engaged to my sister's stepdaughter." He chuckled into his coffee.

Finch and Gabrielle were engaged? Harvey blinked. The blackguard hadn't said a word. His stomach clenched, and he gripped his coffee mug to keep his hands steady.

"Élisabeth is in hysterics. She threw the girl out of the house, and now she's raging that Gabrielle stole things."

"I hadn't heard." This was a good thing for Gabrielle. A very good thing. But the joy he should have felt over her achieving her goal did not come. A dark blankness overtook his soul, spreading until it was difficult to see anything else.

"They're not sure where she's gone. Élisabeth is near ready to hire someone to hunt her down."

"When was this?" Harvey asked.

"Thursday or Friday of last week. They've disowned her, so I don't know why she expects the girl to let her whereabouts be known."

A week ago. And Finch hadn't thought to tell him? So

much for the man wearing his heart on his sleeve. "Why would the parents oppose the match?"

Rouvroy shrugged. "He's English with little fortune yet." He swiped a hand across his mouth. "I thought you were the one she had her eye on at the card party. Must have been wrong."

"Oh, yes. I am nearly engaged myself."

"*Félicitations*," Rouvroy said without enthusiasm.

Harvey rose swiftly, taking out his pocket watch. His brain spun in a way that would not allow him to sit still in this man's presence any longer. He glanced at the watch, but did not register the time. "If you will excuse me, monsieur, I have someone to meet shortly."

"I do not mind at all." That one Rouvroy truly meant.

"Good day to you." He tossed his payment on the table and hurried out into the brazen afternoon. This served him right, finding out about her engagement from someone else, but it felt like an arrow to the heart all the same. He set his course toward the embassy. Finch would know where she was.

As he turned onto the rue Saint-Honoré, a thought burst into his mind. Finch had been dining at Madame d'Épinay's. Yes, that is where she had gone. He turned back around, earning grumbles from the walkers behind him, and hurried in the direction of Madame d'Épinay's house. He didn't know what he would say, but he would not rest until he'd seen her. Knowing she was well after such a distressing experience as being thrown out of her house was all he needed. He would only stay long enough to settle his mind that she was unharmed. Then he would leave, and likely would never see... Well, he wouldn't finish that thought. His heart would not allow it.

CHAPTER 17

"You villain," Harvey said as he entered the library where Gabrielle and Finch sat. "You kept this secret from me all these days when I should have been the first to congratulate you." He hoped his cheerfulness didn't seem too forced.

They both rose to greet him, but Gabrielle would not look him in the eye. Oddly, neither would Finch. Harvey paused. Had he walked into the middle of a quarrel? He hadn't heard any talking in the corridor.

"How very kind of you," Finch said. "We are elated." He couldn't have sounded less certain of what he was saying.

Harvey scrutinized Gabrielle. She wore what looked like an old gown, even older than her blue gown and certainly more worn. Her face was an emotionless mask.

"What are your plans? Will you marry in Paris?" Obviously not if her parents were set against it. A silly question.

"In London," Finch said. "I have written to my mother to make preparations."

"I wish you both joy." He truly meant it. Neither of them seemed joyful.

Finch cleared his throat. "You'll have to excuse me. I have business to attend to on the ambassador's behalf. Barlow, I suppose I might see you this evening." He turned to address Gabrielle. "I will return in time for dinner."

She nodded. He took her hand, kissed it, nodded to Harvey, and then left the library. She folded her hands in front of her, eyes focused on a shelf of books. The soft light filtering through the windows made her skin glow and gave her brown hair a lovely sheen. She was a masterpiece, down to her melancholy green eyes.

"I should find Madame—"

"Wait." He needed to say something. He didn't know what. And he did not want her to go. "Allow me a moment. Please."

She motioned for him to sit, and then sat in the opposite chair. Harvey glanced at the settee she'd indicated. It was the safer option, but his feet carried him to the chair beside hers so they were sitting just as they had when he began teaching her English. She gave no reaction, good or bad.

"How long ago were you forced to leave?" he asked.

"Thursday last."

Just more than a week, then. It wasn't difficult to imagine Madame d'Amilly in a rage. "Were you asking for her blessing?"

"We were not. But she had heard rumors that I was seen kissing an Englishman at the gardens of the Palais-Royal."

Harvey's eyes widened. Someone had seen them? He rubbed the back of his neck. He'd contributed to this. And she sat there telling him in a voice flat as a frozen pond.

"I have settled here well enough," Gabrielle continued,

straightening her posture. "And in June we leave for London."

"Why did you not tell me?" he whispered. A note, a message, anything.

Her eyes narrowed. "I shouldn't be your concern. If Monsieur Finch did not see fit to tell you the news, why would I have?"

They had been working together toward this for weeks. "I thought we were at least friends."

"Yes," she said. But there was a wall there, cold and rigid. She'd relegated him to the same realm as Madame Necker or Lord Stormont.

"Gabrielle, you don't seem well."

She licked her lips. "I wasn't anticipating being thrown out of my home, but the effects of that will fade with time. I am as well as I can be." She straightened her petticoat. "You have your own engagement to worry about."

Acute regret stabbed at his heart. He rubbed at his eyes. What could he say to make it right? Nothing. "I'm deeply sorry. I should have told you."

"Yes, you should have." The slightest waver in her voice belied her own pain.

He reached for her hand, waiting for her to pull away. She didn't. He wrapped his hand around hers. "I want you to be happy. If I could change the way things have turned out, know that I would." Change could bring drastic consequences neither of them wanted to face.

She regarded their hands. "Would you change not telling me or change your engagement?"

Harvey closed his eyes, dropping his head. His engagement. No question. If only love were the most important part of marriage. If only he hadn't agreed to this engagement with Miss Pratt. If only he didn't care about his honor or career.

"I'm happy for you," he said. "I truly am. Finch will treasure you the way you deserve."

"Thank you." It was barely audible. She pulled her hand back, and Harvey released it. He'd overstayed his welcome, if he'd been welcome at all.

"I won't trespass upon your time any longer." He stood, and she rose with him. "If I do not see you before I leave..." His breath hitched. Was this the last time he'd see her? "I wish you all the happiness this world can give." He took her hand once more and pressed his lips to her knuckles, drinking in her scent and her softness one final time. Then he bowed and quit the room, leaving his heart behind.

"Good heavens, child, is everything all right?"

At Madame d'Épinay's voice, Gabrielle brought her head up quickly from the arm of the chair and swiped under her eyes. "Yes!" she cried in the least believable way. Her handkerchief was smeared with rouge from wiping tears off her cheeks.

Madame d'Épinay leaned against the library's doorframe. "You make it easy to believe you."

Gabrielle winced at the sarcasm. She was a terrible liar. "It is only..." What? She had no good excuse. She stifled a shuttering sniff in her handkerchief.

"Come to the kitchen with me. You need to leave this room." Madame d'Épinay herded Gabrielle from the library, with its warm afternoon light, old book scent, and memories of his smile when he taught her to say his name. She trailed obediently behind the older woman, focusing on the cut of the back pieces of Madame d'Épinay's gown. It had been a long time since she'd last made a gown for herself. She might need to use her sewing abilities more often once married to Monsieur Finch.

Focusing on the clothing kept her mind from going back to Harvey's face and the sorrow she'd found there. Distracted, she couldn't remember the feel of his lips on her skin or the way his broad shoulders hunched when she'd asked him if he regretted keeping the truth from her or his engagement. Seeing him downcast had stung so terribly she'd—

No. No, that was exactly what she was not supposed to do. She swallowed the lump in her throat. Her eyes had started to burn again.

"If I did not know better," Madame d'Épinay said, "I would think you were crying over a man."

Gabrielle opened her mouth to respond, but a hiccup answered for her. She clapped a hand over her mouth. She hadn't been crying that hard. Why was she hiccuping?

"Did something happen with Monsieur Finch?" the older woman asked over her shoulder.

"No, of course not." He was everything she'd wanted a month ago. If only she'd realized sooner he wasn't what her heart thought she needed.

"Then someone else?" Madame d'Épinay stopped and turned toward her. "You cannot deny you were crying about a man. The sort of weeping a woman does over a man is quite different from other forms, and it is one I am well acquainted with." She gave a wry smile.

Gabrielle wasn't sure she wanted to know the particulars of those events. She crossed her arms. She couldn't admit to the accusation.

"It is about Lieutenant Barlow, *n'est-ce pas?*"

Gabrielle's face felt as though she'd stuck it in the fire. She put a hand to her cheek, but she couldn't cover her blush. Another hiccup only made the situation more humiliating. It might as well have been an admission.

"He's a handsome man." Madame d'Épinay raised her eyebrows knowingly.

"Yes." Gabrielle groaned internally. She did not want any advice on men from this woman. Not that her previous advice had been bad advice, but as a woman who had plenty of...friends...regardless of marital status, Gabrielle did not trust what she might have to say in regards to marrying one man and loving another.

"That is a conundrum." Madame d'Épinay turned them down a corridor. "Which to choose?"

Gabrielle nearly tripped over her own feet. "*Mais non,* madame! There is no choice. Lieutenant Barlow is engaged."

"Is he?" She clicked her tongue. "And not a word of it to any of us. That does make things a little more complicated."

This was not a conversation she wished to have. She'd had it too many times in her head. "It makes it impossible, not just complicated."

Madame d'Épinay stopped near a window that looked out onto the Parisian streets. Coaches and horses and people mingled in a river of movement, some going north and others going south. Sometimes they'd knock into each other or be forced to stop to avoid collision. Like Gabrielle's muddled mind, there was no order.

"Engaged does not mean married," Madame d'Épinay said with a shrug.

Gabrielle closed her eyes, letting out a long breath. It

might as well mean married. Harvey was a man of his word. He would not go back on it.

"Men are difficult, aren't they?" Madame d'Épinay patted her shoulder. "I've known too many of them in my days, and far too many of them were the boorish sort. And that is why I say if you find a good one, one who respects you, you cannot let him go."

"Monsieur Finch is a good man." She would be happy with him. Eventually. She'd remind herself until she believed it.

"But is he the one you want?" Madame d'Épinay's stare made Gabrielle squirm until she looked away.

"No," she said softly.

"I'm not one to believe there is only one person on the entire earth who could make you happy," Madame d'Épinay said. "But you never know that you weren't thrown together on purpose by some divine providence. If you have any opportunity to realize your dreams, I think you would do well to take your chance.

"Think it over. You will know the right thing to do." The woman squeezed Gabrielle's hands.

Could she still have a chance? Gabrielle's stomach flipped. There was too much at stake and too many things that could go wrong. She could not stand for Harvey to turn her down if she poured her heart out to him. How could she turn her back on Monsieur Finch after all that she had done to catch him and all that he had done to support her when her parents threw her out into the street? She couldn't break his heart or wound his pride.

What if he suspected? Her mouth went dry. Was that why he was so melancholy earlier? A sickening realization settled into her gut. She needed to tell him the truth. Harvey had kept his secret from her, and it had torn her apart, but she was doing the same to Monsieur Finch. How could she admit all that she'd planned and done with Harvey? Her eyes threatened tears again.

Panic rose inside her as the thoughts continued to swirl, intensifying with each rotation through her mind. What would Monsieur Finch do? Would she be alone to rely on Madame d'Épinay's generosity as long as she could? She put a hand to her stomach. The last few days, the future had seemed much clearer. She'd accepted it. Now the questions tumbled about, caught up in the whirlwind.

Madame d'Épinay took her by the shoulders, bringing her thoughts back to the present. "In the meantime, I ordered a fine amount of chocolate from À la Mère de la Famille that was just delivered this afternoon. And since I am the *mère* of the family, I intend to sample it before the rest of the house. Would you like to join me for a cup, even if it is not the breakfast hour?"

Gabrielle nodded, not having words to answer. Chocolate. Yes, chocolate was a good distraction. A way to put off for a moment the looming uncertainty that was her future.

CHAPTER 18

Harvey sighted down the table of the billiards room, twisting a cue back and forth in his hand. He was horrible at this game, but when Lord Stormont had suggested they go for a little respite from the embassy, Harvey jumped at the chance. It seemed all of Paris was waiting for news of Louis XV. Harvey was simply waiting to leave.

The ambassador stood on the opposite side of the table with a mace instead of a cue. The clunky, flat-headed stick was starting to get an old-fashioned reputation, which was why Harvey had selected the cue, but he didn't know that either would have helped him succeed. Give him a nine-pounder and half a gun crew, and he could blow the hat off an enemy seaman several hundred yards away. Hitting these balls around a table with sticks was not something he'd trained for.

"You may not have much more time here, my friend," Stormont said. "I would not waste it overthinking how to hit a billiards ball."

Harvey lined up his cue. "The word on the king does not

seem good." He struck the ball, sending it in a direction he hadn't intended. Blast.

"He has summoned his confessor." Stormont tapped a ball into one of the pockets with his mace. He hit once more and missed.

Even the king had resolved himself to his fate, then. Harvey would have to write to Admiral Pratt. Though he very well might beat the letter back.

"We will both of us be very busy in the next few weeks," the ambassador said. "Colonial uprisings, state mourning, perhaps a promotion."

"Marriage." Harvey attempted to put himself in a better position to hit the ball this time.

"You say it with such foreboding." Stormont laughed. "I take it you are still resolved to carry through with the business contract."

"Nothing has changed my mind on that." But oh, how fate had tried.

"Paris didn't grace you with a little of her magic?"

Yes, she had. Too much of it. "I hardly believe in magic, my lord."

The ambassador tapped his mace thoughtfully against the side of the table. "Perhaps you should. It would do you some good. I cannot help wondering if you were touched by the romance of Paris without knowing it."

Harvey hit the ball, which narrowly missed the pocket. It was closer than he'd hit anything all afternoon, and still he wasn't anywhere near to winning. "If I was, it was fleeting." Even as he said it, he forced back the urge to cringe. It wasn't fleeting at all. He thought about her each day. He missed her laugh and the sound of her saying his name. If he were honest, he would give anything to relive their kiss under the archway.

"Your father is an intelligent man, but not when it comes to love." In the shadowy billiards room, Harvey could not decide whether the man was showing his disappointment or holding in a laugh.

"He was right about this," Harvey said. "Love is not the most important factor in marriage."

"Perhaps not. But trust is."

And Gabrielle had little reason to trust him. Come to think of it, Miss Pratt had little reason to trust him as well. As her soon-to-be intended, Harvey had made other intentions rather clear to someone else. They both deserved better.

"You can be careful when it comes to marriage. You should be." Stormont lifted a cue from its place on the wall and held it up near his old mace. "Times are changing. We do not have to do things in the exact way our parents did them. Sometimes they work, and sometimes they don't."

"Are you not using the mace yourself, and therefore disproving your point?" Harvey folded his arms. He didn't want to talk about Gabrielle any more. The emptiness she'd left in him since their last meeting at Madame d'Épinay's library had festered. If he didn't love her, it wouldn't hurt so much. But he'd already fallen.

"If I didn't use the mace, how else would I give you a chance?" Stormont smirked.

Harvey shook his head as the older man returned the cue to its place. "Some things do not need reinventing."

"Spoken like a true pragmatist."

It wasn't a bad thing to be pragmatic. It was his level head that made him a good officer and it would aid his career as a captain. He leveled his cue for his next turn.

"If you could picture your life in one year, what would it

look like? Austere and cold like your father's?" the ambassador asked. "Or would you find beauty?"

Harvey paused. If it were Downham Cottage, there would be beauty. The natural world always seemed to drift inside the cottage in soft and earthy decorations from the housekeeper. Simple meals and simple company. Views that one could not buy for all the prize money the Crown had to offer. And if Gabrielle could be there to share it, he'd want for nothing.

"Joy is right at your fingertips, Barlow. Will you be the fool and let it drift past? Or will you seize it while you still can?"

Harvey tried to hit the ball, and his cue slid off its smooth surface. He reddened. "That door is closed. She's engaged as well."

The ambassador tilted his head thoughtfully. "You would be surprised at all the things that are still possible at that stage in the process."

"You are suggesting I break off my agreements?" He couldn't do that. He was a man of his word.

Stormont waved a hand. "Not necessarily. I am saying examine your heart and see what you find. From someone who married his wife for love, I would not give that up for status, promotion, or wealth." He took his turn, knocking the last ball into a pocket.

Harvey swallowed. Was he putting promotion above his happiness and Gabrielle's as well? The world would tell him that was the right thing to do. And yet...what if the world was wrong?

"Think on it," the ambassador said, clapping him on the shoulder. "And not to increase your anxiety on the subject, but do it quickly. You may not be here much longer." He sighed. Then he straightened. "Shall we play another game?

I am off to a meeting with Monsieur Borde shortly, but I think I have time to beat you once more."

Gabrielle followed Monsieur Finch to the door after their solemn dinner with Madame d'Épinay. He had been quieter than usual tonight, and she could have sworn his eyes were red-rimmed when he arrived. She dismissed the footman at the door after he'd given Monsieur Finch his hat and cloak so they were alone in the foyer.

He settled the hat onto his head, and she mustered the courage to speak. "You seem troubled, monsieur."

His throat bobbed and his eyes widened. "Troubled?" He dropped his gaze. "Of course I'm not troubled." He fumbled with the tie on his cloak. "There are simply many things happening just now."

"In regards to the king's illness?" she asked.

"The king is not doing well," Monsieur Finch said, speaking with more confidence. "They aren't certain he will last the night."

Her heart twisted. Would Harvey be gone in the morning? She took a deep breath to calm the trembling in her belly. "How horrible."

"It is." The gray twilight seeped in through the windows, lighting his grave expression. "There will be much to do before we leave for London."

"Was that truly why you looked so melancholy this evening?" she asked. She had to get to the subject before she lost her nerve. "You have not seemed yourself these last two weeks."

"I..." He squeezed his eyes shut. "I haven't been."

This was her chance. "You are not happy with our engagement."

He retreated back a step. "Please do not make me answer that question."

She softened her voice. "I think we should be honest with each other. This is one of the biggest decisions either of us will make."

"Don't do this," he begged.

Something was very wrong. What was he not telling her? She bit her lips. He did not desire this engagement, that much was clear, but he was too kind a person to admit it. She would help ease his fears with her own confession. "I've been trying to catch your eye for some time now on purpose to make a match. I wanted someone who would take me away from Paris, and you seemed the most likely option."

"Me?" Monsieur Finch pointed to himself. "Of all the English diplomats, you chose me?"

She nodded. "You seemed the most amiable and willing to overlook my lack of dowry."

He rubbed his brow. "I am most flattered, but there are many with better connections and wealth." She couldn't tell if she detected hurt in his voice as the realization hit that she had tried to use him to escape. It was much the same as when she'd thought Harvey only liked her for her connections.

"Lieutenant Barlow agreed to help me try to win your favor, though I think we were both caught off guard when you told my parents we were engaged." She stared at the floor. One confession made, but there was another, more humiliating one ahead.

"There were rumors about us," he said. "I couldn't let you suffer the consequences. I have more honor than that."

She folded her hands. "I wish to release you from your feelings of obligation. I had insincere motives, and you made your decision without knowing them. I cannot hold you to your word if I have not been honest."

His mouth opened. Hope flickered across his face for the briefest moment. Then he set his jaw. "And leave you to fend for yourself? No. How could I do that?"

"You do not wish for a chance to find love?"

Monsieur Finch dropped his head, the brim of his hat hiding his face. His shoulders hunched, and he looked utterly defeated.

"What is it?" She sensed she'd hit close to the reason for his sorrow tonight. She waited, trying to breathe slowly.

"I do wish for that," he said with a little tremor. "I thought I had found it."

Bile rose to her throat. He'd truly fallen in love with her? She covered her mouth with a hand, dread expanding in her chest.

"She was in agreement. Her parents were in agreement. But her grandfather..."

It wasn't her. She let her hand drop. There was someone else.

"He would not give his blessing and threatened to cut off the rest of the family. She could not do that to them. And a few weeks ago, there was no hope."

That was why he'd turned his attention to her suddenly. He was trying to distract himself. "No wonder you agreed to an engagement so quickly," she said. She could not bring herself to be angry. The poor man was brokenhearted.

He looked up quickly. "Please, do not take offense. We are being honest with each other, after all. I think you a worthy young lady in every way."

She held up her hands to quiet him. "I have not taken offense, monsieur. I am sorry you have dealt with such heartache these last few weeks."

He blew out sharply. "That is not the end of it. Just this afternoon I received…" He pulled a letter from his pocket and held it tenderly before him. His name in a feminine hand graced the outside. "Her grandfather has been convinced of my merits. Lord Stormont interfered on my behalf." He cleared his throat, blinking rapidly. "I do not know why. It is too late."

Gabrielle grabbed his arm, heart leaping. "It is *not* too late. I have already said I would release you from our engagement."

"What will you do?" he asked softly. "You've been thrown out by your parents. You cannot go back to that. And after all the false rumors circulating about that night in the gardens of the Palais-Royal…"

Would the truth convince him? "They weren't as false as you believe." She should be fearful right now, terrified of once again facing an uncertain future, but she wasn't. She released his arm. Whatever the future held, things would work out the way they were meant to. Monsieur Finch would be with someone he loved. And she would have a chance to be.

He watched her, brows knit in confusion, clasping his letter with an iron grip.

"They saw me with Lieutenant Barlow before you arrived." She curled her toes in her shoes, remembering the night. Her face heated. "We did kiss. That is what they saw. Someone assumed it was you." The idea of confusing Harvey for Monsieur Finch would have been laughable if she had not done it once before. "You needn't feel any more guilt on that account."

"Barlow did that?" He tapped the letter against his hand with an expression as though he'd been hit by a coach and could not decipher which way was up.

"We were not as discreet as we thought," she said, raising her hands to her cheeks and willing them to cool.

A flicker of hope touched his eyes. "Why does Barlow not ask you to... Oh." Monsieur Finch winced. "He's practically engaged. That would still leave you on your own."

Would that she could be as sweet as Monsieur Finch, so sorry for another's disappointment even as his impossible dream was coming true. "I will find a way. Do not worry yourself over me. I have friends who will help." Not many, but he didn't need to know that. "I could not live with myself or with you knowing I had prevented the happiness you yearned for."

He seemed to take that in, and Gabrielle watched, attempting to stamp out the dread for fear he'd refuse if he saw her worry.

"I do not know how you can be serious," Monsieur Finch said. "You will bear the brunt of this."

She'd be seen as worthless by Society, unable to keep an engagement after being cast out by her parents. An orphan and a beggar. Gabrielle leveled her shoulders. "I promise that everything will be well with me." This world of finery hadn't ever truly been meant for her. She'd been born a farmer's daughter, and she would find a way back to where she truly belonged, or she would find a new place to belong. If her dearest wish come true, that place would be a little cottage in Sussex.

"Then we have broken our engagement?" he asked timidly.

She nodded, smiling. He shouted in elation, giving her a crushing hug and kissing her cheek. Good heavens! That would bring Madame d'Épinay down the stairs to see what was the matter.

"I cannot thank you enough," he said, releasing her. "If there is anything that you ever need, please ask it. You are welcome at my London house, small as it is, at any time."

"You are very kind."

He beamed brighter than she'd ever seen him before. "Now I am off to the Bordes' to tell them the happy news."

Gabrielle laughed as the awkward meeting at the Palais de Luxembourg suddenly made sense. The cold reception was one of hurt and awkwardness. She could hardly blame Mademoiselle Borde. "Yes, go tell her the good news. And you must give her my apologies."

Monsieur Finch said something that sounded like agreement, but it came out as garbled happiness.

He swung open the front door, and she stopped him before he rushed outside. "Would you do something for me?"

"*Bien sûr*! Anything, mademoiselle."

She wrung her hands. She needed to try before it was too late. "I do not know what Lieutenant Barlow's true feelings are toward me, but would you tell him the situation after you have returned to the embassy from the Borde home? Ask him to come here." Then she could know once and for all if there was any hope for her on that path.

"Yes, I will certainly speak with him." And with that, the ambassador's clerk practically skipped down the steps into the waiting coach. Gabrielle leaned against the doorframe and watched him leave. The weight of their engagement lifted like heavy snow melting in spring. Now she would wait to see what the fates had in store and pray there was some happiness on the horizon.

CHAPTER 19

Once again Gabrielle stood on the front steps of the Hôtel d'Angleterre, knocking on the embassy's door at the break of dawn. She'd waited up most of the night, but Harvey hadn't come. She'd fallen asleep in despair, only to awake with a determination that she would not give up until she'd heard from his own lips he would not change his mind.

At least this time she knew a couple of phrases to charm the grumpy British butler.

The door opened, not to the butler but to Lord Stormont adjusting his wig. He started to say something in English but stopped when his eyes fell on her. "Mademoiselle d'Amilly, I thought you were someone else. I suppose I should start expecting your early visits. I am afraid Finch is still asleep. He did not return until quite late last night, which you are probably aware of as I reckon he was with you."

Gabrielle shook her head quickly. Had Monsieur Finch had a chance to speak to Harvey yet if he'd returned so late? Perhaps she would be giving him the news herself. Relief flooded her. Harvey hadn't just avoided her, then. No reason for despair. "I am not looking for Monsieur Finch but for Lieutenant Barlow."

The ambassador's brow furrowed, then his eyes took on a sorrowful look. "Barlow left half an hour ago."

Gabrielle's heart plummeted. "Where did he go? Perhaps I can wait for him?" She had to speak with him. As soon as possible, or she would go mad.

Lord Stormont rubbed the back of his neck. "He is off to England. The king died in the night."

Her throat tightened, cutting off her breath. No. She was too late. She tried to swallow, tried to speak, but nothing came. He was gone.

"I can find you directions to send him a letter," the ambassador said quickly. "I am terribly sorry, mademoiselle. If I had known you wished to speak to him..." He lifted a hand and let it drop helplessly. He couldn't have known.

The little flame inside her fizzled out. She would write to him, but how soon it would get to him, she could only guess. Not soon enough to prevent making his engagement official.

"*Merci, monseigneur.* I will..." What would she do? There was nothing to do except return to Madame d'Épinay's and attempt to figure out her next plan.

"He did mention stopping for a pastry as he left due to breakfast not being prepared," Lord Stormont said. "Though I do not know which *pâtisserie* he had in mind."

How very Harvey-like to leave after a pastry. A small smile escaped at the same moment as a tear. She swept it away. It wouldn't do to lose her composure in front of the ambassador. He could have gone to any *pâtisserie* in the city, and he might not have stopped for long. She'd never find him.

Unless he went to Stohrer's.

She turned on her heel and raced down the steps.

"Mademoiselle?" Lord Stormont shouted in alarm.

"I think I know where he is," she called over her shoulder, dashing for Madame d'Épinay's coach. She flung open the door. "Take me to Stohrer's on rue Montorgueil. *Rapidement!*" She dragged herself into the coach without help of the steps and fell across the seat. With shaking hands, she pulled the door shut behind her and rapped on the top of the carriage, urging him forward.

The ambassador stood on the front step gaping after her. She lifted a hand in farewell as the coach rattled away across the cobblestone courtyard. Dropping her face to her hands, she murmured a prayer that Harvey would be there. She needed to close this chapter of her life, whatever that ending proved to be.

IT WOULD BE REMISS of me if I did not mention a sudden reluctance toward our negotiations on Eugenia's part. I am certain it is only the natural worry one suffers when faced with a change in circumstances, but I wished to make you aware. Perhaps when you have returned, you will help me to persuade her. Women can always be convinced with a little romance, of which I have no doubt you are as adept as the next lieutenant. She is off to Bath in a few weeks. You will not have long by the time you return. Your reports do not seem to indicate a favorable recovery for Louis XV, but I cannot imagine how long you will remain.

As to the preparations I have mentioned above, I urge you to return the moment you have word. You cannot arrive too soon.

Godspeed,
Admiral Pratt

Harvey sat in a vacant Stohrer's with a half-eaten *baba* before him. He tapped the admiral's folded letter against the table. Outside the purplish morning peeked over the rooftops, unnoticed by the travelers crowding the street. He'd miss it—the hum of Paris, the way the city felt alive, how it filtered into his soul. He'd miss the architecture Finch had taught him to appreciate and crossing verbal swords with *philosophes*.

Most of all, he'd miss her.

His gaze drifted to the empty seat across from him where Gabrielle had sat that first day, admitting her predicament and gaining his help. What he wouldn't give to see her one more time before he left, but it was better this way. As painful as it was to leave without a goodbye, it would be more painful to have her near and not be allowed to hold her in his arms. She was to be another man's wife.

However, he was beginning to doubt he'd be another woman's husband any time soon. He tossed the admiral's letter onto the table, unsure what to make of it. Admiral Pratt wanted him to return and woo Miss Pratt. Clearly the father and the daughter had differing opinions on the match. If she did not want it, that gave Harvey very little motivation to win her over. If only he'd had Finch's luck, with the most wonderful girl in all of Paris trying to win his heart.

The man hadn't returned until after Harvey had gone to sleep, and he didn't rise with the rest of the house when news came of the king's death. Harvey hadn't had a chance to say farewell to the man or wish him luck or threaten to throttle him within an inch of his life if he did anything to hurt Gabrielle.

Harvey sat up. He hadn't realized he'd been slouching. Taking up his fork, he dug into the *baba* once more. A last taste of Paris before the long journey back to England. At least it would feel painfully long. He slipped the bite into his mouth. The sticky pastry didn't taste as delightful this morning as it had all those weeks ago.

He glanced once more at the letter, with Admiral Pratt's pleading to woo his headstrong daughter. How could Harvey court someone when his love for Gabrielle still rumbled in his heart and thoughts of her drifted unbidden through the corridors of his mind?

He couldn't. The realization crashed into him, cold and powerful. He couldn't marry Miss Pratt. It would not be fair to her or to him. Gabrielle had chosen her path, and Harvey likewise could choose. He would choose love, that dream his father had told him was a silly fantasy. Who knew how long it would take to lay his feelings for Gabrielle to rest? He would be patient and let it find him again. As soon as he arrived in England, he would tell the admiral. The man would be furious. Promotions would be delayed. But Harvey would have a clear conscience. At least he would once he overcame his pining.

Harvey swallowed, tracing a line in the table's wood with the tines of his fork. How he wanted to love Gabrielle for all of his days. Clearly God hadn't meant for it to be. If that was so, then Harvey would move forward step by step. He had to trust there was light and happiness ahead. And if by some miracle, Gabrielle... He gave his head a sharp shake. Gabrielle was Finch's. He could not allow himself to entertain wishful thoughts.

The door crashed open, startling him out of his consideration. Like a vision from his dreams, a young woman bounded into the shop. She wore a simple gown and a cap over her hair. She scanned the room, a frantic look on her face, then cried out when she saw him.

"'Arvey!"

The sound of her saying his name made his heart stop. He dropped his fork and jumped to his feet as Gabrielle rushed toward him. What was she doing here? She didn't hesitate but dove into his arms with enough force she sent him stumbling back. A laugh flew from his chest.

"What is this?" He held her, feeling her rapid breathing against his shaking arms like she'd run a long distance.

The shopkeeper hurried into the dining area, but when he saw them together he pivoted and retreated back into the kitchen. Gabrielle didn't seem to notice, and Harvey was too surprised to feel a drop of embarrassment.

"I had to tell you," she said. "Monsieur Finch and I are no longer engaged." A baffling smile lit her face.

Harvey stepped back, keeping hold of her arms. "What did you say?" How had that fool ruined the engagement?

A miracle, something whispered inside him. *You wanted a miracle*.

"He is soon to be engaged to Mademoiselle Borde, and I have no doubt both are quite happy." Gabrielle's green eyes shone.

"That disrespectful turncoat." Harvey hadn't anticipated needing to follow through on the threat he hadn't had the chance to make. "How dare he do this to you." What did this mean? His mind couldn't comprehend what was enfolding before him.

A MATCH GONE AWRY

Gabrielle clamped her hand over his mouth, fingers cool against his lips. "No, 'Arvey. I broke off the engagement."

Harvey frowned. "Why the devil would you do that?" His voice was muffled by her slender hand. After all their work to make the match, she'd thrown it away? His pulse rose. She was free of Finch.

She slowly moved her hand away. "Life is hard enough. I would much rather face it with someone I love." She looked away for a moment, then lifted her chin. "I came to ask if you feel the same."

How could he say all the things he felt? A moment ago she was lost to him forever. Now she stood there with hope glowing on her face, and the more he stared, the deeper he fell. Hers was the face he wanted to come home to after each voyage. The face he'd capture every memory of and hold it in his heart to sustain him through every long and wearying assignment. She was the one he'd love with each breath for the rest of his days.

"I love you, Harvey," she said, emphasizing the H this time and making the corners of his mouth tick upward. "But if you tell me you choose a different path, I will let you leave. I will find my own way." Her voice faltered.

His throat swelled at the precious gift Gabrielle was offering, so full of genuine care and understanding. In his mind he slammed the door on his father's heartless warnings. A new age was dawning, one where love and marriage could walk hand in hand without the ridicule of the world.

"The life I can offer you will not be easy," he said, voice husky. "I will have to leave you."

Gabrielle nibbled her lip and nodded. "I know."

"And you still want that?"

She wrung her hands, eyes not leaving his face. "I want you. We will face the rest together."

He smoothed a lock of hair from her face. He hadn't expected to stumble upon this dream when he'd arrived in Paris. Or more accurately, for this dream to stumble upon him in the Tuileries Gardens. "You will be at the mercy of my sisters when I am on assignment for the navy."

"Do they live near you?"

"Lydia lives just outside the neighboring village."

Gabrielle smiled. "Then I shall finally have sisters of my own. You won't have to worry about me. You see? We can succeed. Please. I love you."

He pulled Gabrielle against him, her hands flying to his waistcoat. He pressed his lips against hers, earning him a little squeal of surprise before she melted into his arms. Gone was the uncertainty from their kiss in the garden. She wrapped her arms around his neck. She'd caught him, completely and thoroughly, and for once he did not mind being the prize.

She leaned back. "Can I take this to mean I am going with you to England?"

He chuckled, kissing her forehead. "How quickly can you gather your things from Madame d'Épinay's?"

"I packed everything last night waiting for you. I was awake most of the night."

He cocked his head. "How was I to know you were waiting for me?" He'd gone to bed early so as to banish the turmoil of confusion for a little while.

"Monsieur Finch said he would tell you." She winced as though she were the one who had forgotten to inform him.

Harvey groaned. If that man's head were not secured to his shoulders, he would not remember to bring it with him. He had apparently lost it last night. "Finch is incredibly lucky you chased me down this morning."

"*I* am the lucky one," she said, kissing his cheek before

laying her head on his shoulder. And in that moment, though the world was tossed with chaos, threatening to burst, Harvey could not help but feel that everything was right. He rested his head atop hers and squeezed her tightly. "*Je t'aime*," he whispered.

"Shall we leave?" she asked.

He nodded. "Let's go home, *mon amour*."

EPILOGUE

Five months later

Gabrielle didn't know if she'd ever get used to how green the English countryside was. She hadn't been anywhere this vibrant since her childhood home in the countryside. Though this land was so far from that lovely French countryside she'd once known, somehow this little corner of Sussex had quickly come to feel like home.

This morning she sat on the bench in their little garden behind Downham Cottage, her cloak pulled snuggly around her. The autumn air brushed her cheeks. It would warm by midday, but at this hour she could detect the hint of winter chill. She closed her eyes and reveled in the fresh scent of leaves and grass mixed with the earthy notes of soil the servant had just turned over in the vegetable beds. Six months ago she couldn't have imagined this sort of simple freedom.

"English ladies like to sleep in, you know."

Gabrielle turned at her husband's voice as he came up

the path behind her. "No more than French ladies," she said.

"I suppose I wouldn't know." He sat on the bench beside her, then nudged her a little to make room. It left her pressed against his side, forcing him to put his arm around her. "My French lady likes to get up at daybreak."

"Good morning, *capitaine*," she said, mixing her English and French. Gracious. She could never remember how to say that word in English.

"Cap-ee-TEN," Harvey teased, mimicking her French pronunciation. "I'm not really a captain, remember? I'm still a lieutenant."

Gabrielle huffed. In name. He'd been appointed to command a little guard ship at the mouth of the Thames, one that he claimed was not large enough to warrant an advancement. Admiral Pratt had not been pleased by his refusal to marry Miss Pratt. Harvey did not know when a promotion would come. Until then, she would appreciate the lack of advancement keeping him close to England. "Do you command a ship?"

"It depends who you ask," he said. "A sloop is not always considered a ship."

More confusing than English itself were all these ranks of people and ships. Not to mention the names. She'd never keep them straight. "Does your crew call you captain?"

He sighed. "Yes, but that doesn't mean I have advanced to the rank of captain. I am just Lieutenant Harvey Barlow when not in command."

She shrugged. "Then you are close enough to being a captain to me. You protect the Thames very well." Some sort of insect buzzed through the field of grass in the direction of the hill that rose on the north side of the cottage.

Lavender shadows still reached most of the way up the hill, but a tiny sliver of gold kissed its round head.

"How do you know I do it well?" Harvey took her hand and brought it to his lips, his warm breath tickling her skin.

"I have not come across any angry colonists since you left." It earned her a laugh, the kind she missed greatly the two months he'd been gone. That would change in less than two weeks when she returned with him to London at the end of his leave. She wouldn't get to see him every day, but it would be nice to see him more often through the winter. She would miss their little sanctuary at Downham Cottage, though.

"There is time for that still." Worry touched the corners of his eyes.

She wrapped both arms around his. "No need to fret over that now. We have more than a week before we have to leave. Until then, you are mine."

He chuckled and kissed her temple, sending a tingle from her head to her toes. It felt like a dream to have him here in this tiny corner of paradise, where the style of her clothing and the way she carried herself did not matter. Perhaps someday he would take more of an interest in farming than captaining. Until then, she could not think of a place she'd rather be.

"Do you think we will meet the Finches in London?" she asked. It would be nice to see a fellow countrywoman, someone with whom she could laugh about the English and their odd customs. She loved England, but sometimes she missed France more than she had anticipated. Mademoiselle Borde—Mrs. Finch—might help that. Gabrielle had written to her father a few times but had received no answer, so she could not look forward to regular letters from home for the time being. She could only pray that someday that changed.

"I heard Lord Stormont was requesting the Finches' return to Paris," Harvey said. "Perhaps we might dine with them before they leave."

She mumbled her agreement with that plan. "That reminds me. Lydia wished for us to dine with them tonight," she said, enjoying the touch of his lips far too much as he continued to place little kisses on her temple.

"Must we?" he murmured against her brow.

"Harvey! How horrible. Of course we must." His sister was already put out that they were leaving.

He encircled her in his arms, his lips moving past her cheekbone. "It would be far better if we simply stayed in tonight, *mon amour*."

She laughed as his lips covered hers, gently and playfully trying to persuade her to decline his sister's invitation. It was tempting, to be certain. Lydia had no doubt invited several guests, which would make for a crowded dinner. But they had to go. She would miss her sister-in-law when they left, and there would not be many more opportunities to see Lydia or her family before then.

"We simply must," she said, pulling away and cupping his face in her hands.

"And why is that?"

She set her face with a serious expression. "Lydia intends to play cards tonight, and it has been far too long since I have beaten you at cards." She giggled at his sour expression.

"I might win this time, you know."

She shook her head. "Never."

"You stole my heart and now you intend to steal my

dignity at the card tables." He pulled her closer until she nestled against his shoulder.

"You said when we married that the only thing I could not steal from you was your pastries." She gave an innocent shrug.

He sighed. "I suppose I can content myself with that." He smoothed a little wisp of hair that fell along her neck.

"*C'est bon*," she said, "because I am about to steal a kiss."

And he let her, grinning from ear to ear, with all the grace a new husband could muster.

La fin

Author's Notes

While the original publication year for *Conversations of Emilie* was 1774, I could not find an exact date, and therefore used some creative license to put it within the timeline of this story. The conversation tarts were originally made to celebrate this book, and they are still available to purchase at many Parisian pastry shops, though it is unclear who actually invented them.

Lord Stormont, the Necker family, Madame d'Épinay, d'Alembert, l'Abbé Raynal, Monsieur Gabriel are all real people. While I have tried to create them on the page in a way that is true to their character, some creative liberties have been taken.

Madame Necker was one of the famous *salonistes* who hosted the famed *philosophes* for weekly get-togethers. Madame Necker held her salons on Friday evenings and also hosted a more intimate dinner on Tuesday for her closest friends.

All the places my characters visit are real places. The old embassy is now a hotel and the house the d'Amilly family rents (formerly rented by the Necker family) is a private

AUTHOR'S NOTES

residence. Stohrer's is one of the oldest *pâtisseries* in Paris, though a little artistic liberty was taken to give it more of a café or tea house feel. À la Mère de la Famille is an 18th century chocolatier and confectioner that has been in business since 1761. You can visit both of these original stores in Paris today. Likewise Café de la Régence was a real 18th century coffee house that survives today as a restaurant. It is located near the Palais-Royal.

Iphigénie en Aulide premiered on April 19, 1774 at the Salle du Palais-Royal as portrayed in the story. While this opera house burned down later in the 18th century, the gardens are still open to guests.

There is evidence from journals that Lord Stormont attended the Neckers' salon but how frequently is unknown. Artistic liberty was taken to make him a frequent visitor.

Louis XV died of smallpox in May of 1774. Doctors at the time believed that he had previously contracted smallpox and therefore would recover, but he likely suffered from a different disease as a child. All theories about his health in this book are based on beliefs from the time period.

Much of my research on the *philosophes* and Neckers are from *The Salon of Madame Necker* by the Vicomte d'Haussonville, which includes many snippets of journals and letters. I only scratched the surface of this fascinating topic, and I wish I had more time to dive into the interesting personalities of these men and the women who ran the salons they frequented.

Acknowledgments

When my dear friend Jennie Goutet reached out to me with the idea for this series, I was instantly delighted. Paris has been such an important part of my life, and the time I spent there was a season of growth, excitement, and even romance. It was a place I hadn't yet brought into my works in a significant way. What's more, the idea of participating in such a fun multi-author project with a friend who has helped me so much with my French Revolution novels made any other response but yes impossible. Jennie's vision from the beginning has been spectacular, and I'm so grateful she extended the invitation. I'm so proud of all the work our group has put in to make this series what it is, and I'm grateful, as always, for her help with French, research, and beta reading.

I'd never met Christina Dudley or Sofi Laporte before they joined our group, and it has been wonderful getting to know them and their work as we exchanged research, plotted our stories, and planned our marketing. I couldn't have asked to be part of a better group of ladies for this project.

A lot of crazy things happened in the months leading up to the publishing of *A Match Gone Awry*. Lots of career changes, family emergencies, and general craziness. Deborah M. Hathaway was there through it all, listening to my worries and complaints. I'm so grateful for a friend and critique partner like her.

A huge thank you to my critique group—Joanna Barker, Heidi Kimball, and Megan Walker—for their encouragement and help in working through the difficult aspects of this story. Their grasp of storytelling never ceases to amaze me. Love you ladies!

I'm so grateful to my beta readers for their feedback on this book. Thanks to Sam Haysom, Sharleen Roberts, Corie Hawks, Deborah M. Hathaway, Joanna Barker, A. L. Sowards, Karen Thornell, Rebekah Isert, Jennie Goutet, and Christina Dudley for their help getting this story ready for the world.

I am most appreciative of my friend Rachel Bergquist's help with the details of Gabrielle's wardrobe and the dress altering scene. She is so knowledgeable about historical fashion and clothing construction, and her work is inspiring!

Shout-out to Shaela Kay Odd, who designed our gorgeous covers. She brought our (mostly Jennie's) vision of a little taste of Paris to life, and we couldn't be happier with her work. And a shout-out to Christopher Sorensen and the Chathams, whose research advice I somehow always need, even when my books aren't set at sea.

I'm forever grateful to my wonderful family for their love and support, especially to Jeff. I couldn't have finished this mad dash of drafting and editing multiple books at the same time without his willingness to pick up the slack and shoulder more of the responsibilities than usual. And thanks to my four kids who are my biggest fans. I love you all.

Most of all, thank you to a Heavenly Father who gave me a passion and desire to try to make the world a little more beautiful through the telling of stories. I hope I have spread a bit of that light with *A Match Gone Awry*.

The *Georgians in Paris* frolics continue with
The Vicomte's Masquerade!

He's the last man she'd ever marry. She's the last woman he'll ever love.

Sent to Paris with her elderly chaperone, Miss Melinda Finlay resists her arranged marriage to a haughty French vicomte. The headstrong beauty would rather drown in the channel than marry the odious man! Fate intervenes when a dashing Scottish traveler crosses their path, offering assistance and a carriage ride to Paris. Little does Mellie know that this charming stranger carries his own burden of hidden truths.

As their enchanting adventure unfolds amidst the splendor of the Tuileries and Versailles, Mellie and Philippe discover a passionate connection that neither anticipated. Yet, as the shadow of Mellie's impending nuptials looms over them, she faces an impossible choice. Will she have the audacity to defy the shackles of societal convention and follow her heart?

BOOKS IN THE GEORGIANS IN PARIS SERIES:

The Accidental Servants by Christina Dudley
A Match Gone Awry by Arlem Hawks
The Vicomte's Masquerade by Sofi Laporte
A Sham Betrothal by Jennie Goutet

Also by Arlem Hawks

Georgana's Secret

Beyond the Lavender Fields

Along a Breton Shore

Across the Star-Kissed Sea (October 2024)

The Steadfast Heart

All You Wish

In Pursuit of a Gentleman

Commander of His Heart

A Lady's Wager (The Diamond of Bristol)

About the Author

Arlem Hawks began making up stories before she could write. Living all over the Western United States and traveling around the world gave her a love of cultures and people, and the stories they have to tell. She graduated from Brigham Young University with a degree in communications and emphasis in print journalism, and now lives in Utah with her husband and four children.

Printed in Dunstable, United Kingdom